PEACE

ON THE

WESTERN

FRONT

Mattia Signorini holds a degree in communications from the University of Padua. After working as an Editor in Milan, he started a creative writing school, the Palomar School, in his hometown, Rovigo. He also founded and directs the yearly literary festival RovigoRacconta. He debuted in 2007 with Lontano da ogni cosa (Far From Everything), followed by La Sinfonia del Tempo Breve (The Symphony of the Nineteenth Century), Ora (Now), Le Fragili Attesi (Fragile Awaitings), and Stelle Minori (Lesser Stars). He is the winner of the Premio Tropea 2010, and finalist of the Premio Stresa.

Peace on the Western Front is the first of a trilogy he is planning on themes of world peace.

PEACE
ON THE
WESTERN
FRONT

MATTIA SIGNORINI

**MANILLA
PRESS**

First published in the UK in 2023 by
MANILLA PRESS
An imprint of Bonnier Books UK
4th Floor, Victoria House, Bloomsbury Square, London, England, WC1B 4DA
Owned by Bonnier Books
Sveavägen 56, Stockholm, Sweden

A CIP catalogue record for this book is
available from the British Library.

ISBN: 978-1-78658-341-3

Also available as an ebook and an audiobook

1 3 5 7 9 10 8 6 4 2

Typeset by IDSUK (Data Connection) Ltd
Printed and bound in Great Britain by Clays Ltd, Elcograf S.p.A.

FSC
MIX
Paper from
responsible sources
FSC® C018072
www.fsc.org

Manilla Press is an imprint of Bonnier Books UK
www.bonnierbooks.co.uk

A hero is no braver than an ordinary man, but he is brave five minutes longer.

– Ralph Waldo Emerson

Foreword by A N Wilson

This short tale is one of the most profound things recently written about the wickedness and folly of war. It centres round the symbolic moment, Christmas 1914, when the opposing armies in the trenches near Ypres joined in a chorus of the carol 'Silent Night' and subsequently laid down their arms for a day.

The propaganda from the British government had told everyone that the war would be over by Christmas. When the men on the Western Front – Germans and English together – began to sing a Christmas carol, they were giving their own response to this monstrous lie. When they began to play football together, rather than fire bullets, they made one of the most eloquent statements in modern history.

Here we read of William Turner, a young English soldier who initiated that truce. In this story, he had already had an encounter with a young German soldier, Carl Mühlegg, in a forest near Ypres. The German boy could have shot the English boy, who was trying to rescue a local girl – the Girl with the North Sea in her Eyes, as they nicknamed her. William wants to take her to the sea, and by rescuing her, he reminds his German counterpart, Carl, of the sane world outside the theatre of war, where human beings do not define one another as violent fighting units to be shot at, but are living, breathing, feeling individuals, capable of love.

'I don't think life is what happens to you. Maybe it's nothing more than our reaction to those circumstances,' says Carl to William. And, years later, when he is bringing his son to revisit the scenes of these wartime encounters, he says to his boy, 'He' – i.e. William – 'showed me and many other men the way to peace.'

Carl says this to his son in the early 1930s. He remembers a corporal who (in this story, if not in actual history) had acted as a messenger between the front line and the regimental headquarters. This young man, who had won the Iron Cross, was now, in 1933 – when Carl is telling the story to his son – the Chancellor of Germany, and he had learned none of the lessons which were so obvious to Carl, to William, and to the other young men who laid down their weapons and played football together, rather than kill. His name, it scarcely needs pointing out, was Adolf Hitler.

It was inspired of Mattia Signorini to make Hitler part of the story. As we know from hindsight, all those who supposed during the 1930s that Hitler would have brought peace to Europe, if only certain conditions were fulfilled, were deluding themselves. If only France could give up its demand for German reparation . . . If only Germany could be allowed the Sudetenland . . . If only, if only, Herr Hitler would not be 'compelled' to go to war. We realise, however, that Hitler saw himself, the former dispatch rider, as a mighty warrior, and war was his raison d'être. While his credulous subjects in Germany hailed an economic miracle, they did not realise that the miracle was based on turning German industry into a war machine. Factories such as Volkswagen were entirely devoted to building armaments, tanks, planes, in readiness for Hitler to show himself as one of the great military leaders in history, in succession to Frederick the Great or Napoleon.

Why do men go to war? (We use the word 'men' in that sentence because it always is men who do it.) The greatest book ever written about war – Homer's *Iliad* – depicts Ares, the God of War (whom the Romans called Mars) glutting himself on human blood, while the other gods stir up strife, persuading human beings that it will be in their best interests to solve their differences and difficulties by acts of slaughter. By some mysterious process, successive governments throughout history have persuaded young men that it would be in their city's or nation's interest for them to take up weapons and kill other young people whom they have never even met.

In a sense, every piece of war literature since has simply been a footnote to the *Iliad*. Every act of war has simply been a repetition of the pointless interchange of mass murder on the plains of Troy.

For war is murder. The wonderful scene in this story, when William persuades Carl, in the forest, that there is nothing normal or natural about their pointing guns at each other, and preparing to kill each other merely because one is German and the other English. But, for their governments at home, the lunacy of war has become the only sanity. Those young men – or boys – who see what an evil, malicious and dishonest business war always is are either hastily transferred behind the lines or are actually shot.

The famous Christmas Truce of 1914 was the one day of the war when sanity surfaced. 'The moment we lay down our arms, war ceases to exist.' Both our young men – Carl and William – know this to be the case. The Christmas game of football between the Tommies and the Jerries makes that abundantly clear. For a moment, it looks as if the sanity of the ordinary young person has triumphed over the truly wicked insanity of the world governments – Britain, Germany, Russia, France. The game of football on Christmas Day was the most anarchic, subversive thing that the Western governments had encountered.

It is imperative for these governments, as soon as Christmas Day is over, to insist on 'business as usual'. The killing must recommence. Those who played football and witnessed the scene of the 'little peace' are too numerous to be executed, as individual awkward customers are. But they can be sent to other parts of the theatre of war. The incident can be buried. Digging more trenches, and encouraging more and more young men to kill one another, is represented, on both sides, as the highest possible virtue.

Four years before the outbreak of the First World War, the greatest war writer since Homer, Lev Nikolayevich Tolstoy, had died in Russia. We remember him as the author of *War and Peace*. The thousands who followed his coffin to a grave near his home Yasnaya Polyana ('Bright Glade'), watching it buried in a simple turf plot, probably contained only a few who had read *War and Peace*, his magnificent analysis of the insanity of the Napoleonic conflicts. But they had read his pacifist writings: *The Kingdom of God is Within You, What Then Must We Do?* and many others. Tolstoy had warned the world that government itself was based on violence, and that if the arms race which had begun in the 1890s continued, there would be a catastrophic global war from which the world would never recover. He was right. Greatest of novelists, greatest of prophets.

When I read Mattia Signorini, I kept thinking of Tolstoy. This short tale has much in common with Tolstoy's writings, and its message is the same. But, at the time of writing, there are wars raging in the Middle East, in the Ukraine, in East Africa. There seems little prospect of governments, which depend on violence – literally – for their lifeblood, listening to the message of peace which this story contains.

A N Wilson, July 2023

ONE

Flanders, 1933

DECEMBER 1933. A MAN and a boy were walking down a country lane in Ypres.

They had travelled all day, taking the train to Brussels and another to Ypres, a small town of less than three thousand inhabitants. They had eaten a simple snack in a local coffee shop and the manager tried, unsuccessfully, to understand what language they were speaking; it sounded familiar. 'Germans,' a customer had said before watching them leave.

They walked until sunset, until the man pointed southwards and said to the boy, 'We're almost there. And then we can sleep.'

They came off the path and descended a slope of frosty grass. The boy walked faster now. He had grown a few inches in the past couple of months and his soft facial features were now more pronounced. The man was carrying a burlap sack – their only piece of luggage – on his shoulders; it wasn't that heavy. When they reached the inn, they banged their boots together to shake off the dirt.

The owner led them inside and then into a room with a double bed and a wooden wardrobe. The man took off his hat with his good hand and, with his stump, he gestured to the boy. The boy ran his hand over the mattress and lay down.

Once it was completely dark, the man took out a candle from his bag and clutched it, half-closing his eyes. He moved his lips ever so slightly, as if reciting a silent prayer, before placing the candle on the windowsill. He looked wistfully out at the valleys, barely perceptible in the fading evening light.

They ate two leftover pretzels for dinner. The man asked the boy if he was cold, and the boy nodded. He handed him a jumper and then stretched out on the neat bed, fully clothed.

The next day they rose at dawn and set off after each drinking a glass of milk. They carried two sandwiches they had bought from the innkeeper for their lunch. For almost an hour they walked through fields, tightly wrapped in their woollen overcoats. Suddenly the man stopped. The boy looked around and noticed that the grass had given way to trenches of dark earth, no deeper than two feet, that stopped and started up again a little further on.

'This is the place,' said the man. 'It's been years since I was first here. I was nineteen, not much older than you. I was in trenches that were similar to the ones you can see now. I'd have my rifle at the ready, without knowing if I'd live to see the next day.'

'You had to defend yourself?'

'From men I didn't know.'

'How many of you were there?'

'Thousands.'

The number ran through the boy's head – *thousands.* He grimaced.

'I can't imagine a number that big.'

'I couldn't either, till I saw it with my own eyes.'

'Was it scary?'

'Very.'

The man then explained to the boy that he had wanted to come back here because he had made a promise concerning a young man. That he had already put off this journey for too long.

'What did the young man do?' asked the boy.

'He taught me that when everything seems to be going against us and we feel like there's no way out, it's still possible to make a choice. Those words saved my life.'

The man motioned for the boy to sit down. The boy hoisted himself onto the earthen wall, his legs dangling, tapping his feet against the packed mud.

'D'you want to know his story?'

The boy nodded.

The man knelt down and ran his palm over the edge of the rocky grass. He glanced fleetingly at the gold watch on his wrist and looked up at the blue sky as it gradually filled with clouds.

'To tell you, I'll have to start from the beginning.'

'All right,' said the boy.

'His name was William Turner. He came here in the autumn of 1914 believing, like all of us, that the war would be over by Christmas. When he arrived, he didn't know what it meant to fight, or what a battlefield was.'

'I don't understand why he came, then.'

'He had to keep a promise, too.'

The boy came and sat next to his father.

'And what was the promise, Dad?'

Flanders, 1914

WILLIAM TURNER ARRIVED ON the outskirts of Ypres one afternoon in early December 1914. After a few days' journey on two trains and a ferry, he had marched across the roads of Belgium with a dozen other young volunteers.

The third line was an hour's walk from the front, which had carved the town into two halves. On one side were the Germans and on the other, the Belgian, French and British armies, whom William was proud to have just joined.

William paused to look at the thick smoke rising in the distance from the bombs, darkening the sky. He thought that soon he would be on the battlefield. He tried to imagine it as he had done impatiently every day for weeks. At the same time, he was aware of a feeling of emptiness rising from the pit of his stomach. He began to walk again, swiftly, and soon reached the line of new recruits.

The camp had been set up around an old factory. Some soldiers were busy building fences while others shifted scrap metal and bricks in carts. In the distance, William saw two nurses emerging from what must have been a large warehouse. He was surrounded by barren earth and leafless trees.

He waited his turn in the forecourt and eventually found himself face to face with a priest dressed in a tunic. Before saying anything, the priest reached for his half-pint mug of beer, took a gulp, and put it down on the table.

'Soldier, find a bunk and settle in.' He handed William a coarse woollen blanket and a sheet of paper with numbers on, then pointed to a barn that had been hastily converted into a dormitory. Then, as if he had forgotten something, he added, 'Father Adams, at your service.'

William glanced at the blanket.

'It's all holey.'

'It has already kept other soldiers warm – those who served their country before you. You should be proud of that, soldier.'

'I guess they're at the front now.'

'If God hasn't already taken them. Settle in, then get in line for your ration,' Father Adams said, handing another equally holey blanket and sheet of paper to the soldier behind William.

William crossed the forecourt. At the entrance, the soldier standing guard was taking notes in his register. He took William's piece of paper, arching an eyebrow while he read.

'This is dormitory number five. It's where you'll sleep . . . Over there at the end – follow me. It says Turner here, right?'

'Yes. Private.'

They walked among the cots dividing up the room into long rows. Some beds were made of straw, others were rags layered one on the top of the other. The soldier studied the register closely.

'Here, bunk number 179 is yours. Treat it well.' He pointed past the entrance door. 'The ration line's over there. You'd better hurry if you want to eat.'

'Bunk number 179 and the ration.'

'Correct.'

'What's your name, soldier?'

'Foster, welcome attendant.'

'Private Foster, a question.'

'Ask me.'

'What's it really like – the war?'

Foster arched an eyebrow again. His face turned grim in concentration.

'Grey,' he said.

William laid the torn blanket over his cot and took off his rucksack. He fished out his notebook from his pocket, leafed through it and paused at the page where he had written:

EQUIPMENT

He went through the list, carefully checking each entry:

Uniform that's still in good condition.

'Wearing it.'

Wool cap.

He brought his hands to his head.

'On my head.'

Boots with laces.

'On my feet.'

Box of cartridges.

'Here.'

Aluminium cup, cup, spoon, pen, emergency tin of meat, two emergency packets of biscuits, emergency tin of peas, emergency chocolate bar, first-aid medication, change of woollen sweater, spare woollen jumper, two pairs of underpants, one black, one blue, grey scarf, and a watch.

'Carrying them.'

Belt.

'Wearing it.'

Notebook.

'Got it in my hand.'

Identity badge with William Turner, Private, 28 military postcards, crumpled but proudly kept British flag, camera.

'I've got everything, or almost.'

He stuck his hand inside the rucksack and rummaged for a minute, searching for the three ounces of ham he had managed to save from his journey. It wasn't there; someone on the train or ferry had probably stolen it while he was sleeping. He picked up his bowl and spoon and determinedly made his way back to the forecourt, rucksack in tow. The ground outside was swollen with rain.

He found a small group of soldiers nearby. He heard one of them ask for another ration. A burly man with thick body hair was standing behind a table, on top of which were several pots; all bar one was empty.

'Go ahead – this is all I've got left for the others.'

The *others* were, in this order: a small man with round glasses, probably in his thirties or forties; a young man, about the same age as William; and William himself, gripping his mess tin.

He ate alone under an iron pergola, listening to the rain as it mingled with the sound of soupy stew dripping from the spoon into the bowl each time he brought it to his mouth. If there was one thing that put him at peace with the world, it was the sound of steadily falling rain, bouncing off roofs and the road. It was like listening to a piece of music. William savoured these moments of stillness; soon he would be at the front.

He had read about the front in the papers: it was the ultimate resistance against the enemy; the trenches must be defended at all costs. William couldn't wait to get there.

He took out his camera. Closing one eye, he used the other to observe his surroundings. He wanted to find something – a person, an object – that would one day remind him of his first day as a soldier. He ended up fixing his gaze on a long, threadbare rag hanging from a nail on a wooden wall. It reminded him of his mother mending her customers' clothes in their small kitchen: she, too, would hang the clothes on a nail in the wall before settling down to work. She would stare at the material for a few minutes, as if deciphering the secret of the perfect repair. Each piece of clothing had one, she always told William.

He released the shutter, put the camera away and looked up at the sky. Big, dark clouds were gathering.

'Grey,' he said to himself.

*

Ever since the summer of 1914, in the United Kingdom they'd spoken about the war as if it was a great adventure. Hardly anyone listened to the pacifists' opposition to the war.

The German army had crossed the borders into neutral Belgium without facing any serious obstacles. On 20 August it entered Brussels; on the 25th it devastated the city of Leuven, setting fire to the houses of civilians and the old university, and anyone who didn't manage to escape was shot on the spot. In September, dozens of women were arrested and killed in Aarschot. Two months later, the Germans had almost reached the North Sea.

William had seen the North Sea only once before he went to war, with his father and mother when he was a child. He had thought about it ever since. He liked to imagine that the sea was made from long, endless rains a thousand years ago. He imagined how it had sounded, the rain when it first hit dry earth, then the wet earth, and then finally as it continued to pour for two or three generations, on to more rain that had now become the sea. The North Sea.

If the German army had reached the sea, they would have blocked the flow of supplies and soldiers, and the English wouldn't have had much of a choice. The conquest of Paris would have been imminent, and the Allies would be remembered as the defeated and not the stalwart defence. The allied generals' plan was to stop the German army as soon as possible and end the war by Christmas. They tried, and succeeded in halting the advancing Germans. But they met unexpected, continuous and fierce resistance which soon wore them down.

This had all happened at the end of October, as William was walking listlessly down the street, delivering packages to his father's customers. The armies were battling near Ypres, a small textile town which was beginning to crumble under the bombing. When the German army was nearing victory and preparing to march towards the North Sea, something else had happened.

It concerned the sluices on the Yser River, a four-hour walk from Ypres, and two men: the tiny guard, Karel Cogge, who knew every inch of that countryside, and the mighty sailor, Hendrik Geeraert, as strong as an ox. While thousands of men relentlessly fought against one another on the battlefields, Cogge and Geeraert served their country. Cogge had begun searching in the grass for the key for the gate to open the sluices; he found it. Geeraert took it from him, turning it forcefully until he managed to loosen the nut. At high tide, an enormous wave of seven hundred thousand cubic metres of seawater poured on to the fields of Flanders. The sea, thought William, as he read the news report. It's always the sea. The water turned Flanders into a swamp, flooding cultivated fields, inundating farms and houses. Thus, the German army found itself in a serious stalemate.

When William finished reading, an advertisement at the bottom of the page caught his attention. A few words:

Your country needs you.

It went on to claim that England urgently needed volunteers, that they would save thousands of lives, that the war would be over by Christmas.

The prospect of saving all those lives ran through William's mind as he finished his last delivery and returned to his father's workshop. He, too, could enrol, cross the sea and travel to Ypres. If he saved even one person's life, he would keep the promise he'd made to his mother on her deathbed all those years ago. He could make amends with fate.

'With all the work to be done around here, all you can think about is leaving?' came his father's response. He didn't even look up from his workbench. William mumbled something about his mother, who was resting in her grave. 'Because of you, William . . .' his father retorted, but

William didn't wait for him to finish and went out onto the road, where a cold wind was blowing, clamouring for winter to come.

If his father was a season, he would be winter. William would have liked to do something – anything – to melt his frozen heart, but he knew that his father blamed him. He blamed him every day, in his silences, in the way he always avoided William's eyes, except for fleeting moments. If William stayed with his father at the shop, he, too, would gradually freeze over.

This was what William thought as he walked briskly towards the military barracks with his hands in his pockets. It was time to get even. War is the only way to bring about peace: that's what the papers said.

And William Turner desperately needed peace.

He enrolled in the army that same day.

William signed up outside the barracks, in a huge square, where officers sat on makeshift benches taking the aspiring soldiers' details. At the far end of the square, soldiers and a few officials watched a large number of young men shooting at cardboard cut-outs. The officers asked William three questions: What's your name? Why d'you want to enlist? What d'you imagine yourself doing?

Without thinking too much, he replied to the second question saying that he wasn't the type to sit around with his hands in his pockets. To the third, trying to anticipate what he thought they wanted to hear, he said calmly, 'Shoot.'

'You'll make a good rifleman,' responded an officer, whose name William would soon forget. He placed a rifle in William's hand.

'This is a glorious Lee–Enfield rifle. There are only three rules – hold with nerves of steel, aim with nerves of steel, shoot with nerves of steel. Try that cut-out over there.'

William lifted, aimed, and fired relentlessly. Even though his bullets never even came close to the silhouette for an entire week, he wasn't discouraged. By the middle of the second week, one shot out of every ten hit the target. When he finished training a few days later, he had doubled his score.

'Two shots out of ten is a good start,' said the officer. 'You're a real rifleman now. Tomorrow you'll get on a train and go and serve your country.'

William held his rifle tightly, even now as he lay on his bunk, waiting for someone to give him a task or tell him when he would leave for the front.

In the middle of the afternoon, Foster, the welcome attendant, came into the dorm, straightened up and brought his hands brusquely to his sides. 'All recruits to the square for assembly with Major Weasel.'

William jumped to his feet without letting go of the rifle, picked up his rucksack and followed his comrades who, like him, had just arrived. They all wore the same expression of enthusiasm and uncertainty.

Foster announced Major Weasel, who emerged from a stone shelter. Smoke was rising out of the roof. It was probably the major's living quarters. After pulling down his jacket, and adjusting the lonely strips of hair hanging from the sides of his head, he stood in the middle of the square and stared at the newcomers. His beady black eyes looked everywhere and nowhere, just like those of a weasel.

'Soldiers, a godforsaken little place like Ypres has become the centre of this world, and you are part of it!' he said. 'Soon you'll be at the front – it's only a few hours' walk away. There, you'll follow one simple rule – shoot every German who comes within range. And above all, remember that under no circumstances must you run away like rabbits. If anyone even thinks about it, I'll personally order your execution. Is that clear?'

'All clear,' replied the soldiers.

'You'll stay there for a fortnight. After that, other soldiers will arrive to relieve you. In the meantime, Foster will assign you your tasks.'

The young men were herded into a long line; at the end of it was Foster, frowning as if he was trying to calculate the result of a complex mathematical equation. He opened a page of the register containing the list of new arrivals. For those who could glimpse it, the list looked like endless railway tracks.

All they could hear was the rain; the same rain that had fallen on the North Sea over so many lifetimes, thought William. Foster's gaze had softened. One could almost make out the hint of a satisfied smile at the corners of his mouth; he had worked out his equation.

He called out the names of some of the soldiers and they stepped forward. Twenty in total. They would assist in the field hospital. 'Where the most severely wounded struggle between life and death,' he said, as if it was quite normal to struggle between life and death in a converted cow barn in the war.

William let the idea of death circle around his head like a spinning top while he waited for his task. The same sense of emptiness he'd felt when he had arrived grew in his belly – and this time he knew it was fear.

'Don't pay it any mind, William,' he said to himself. 'You made the right choice, enlisting.'

'Turner, I said to move forward with Martin. Are you deaf?' Foster repeated.

Edgar Martin was the little man with round glasses whom William had met the day before, while they queued for food. He was so tiny that even his small uniform looked too big for him.

William and Martin were to explore the surrounding areas, especially the houses, with another five pairs of soldiers. Foster gave each of them a map with hand-drawn directions. Their assigned spot was a three-hour walk away.

'We believe that they've been abandoned, but you never know. Take what you can and make a list of what you can't carry. Other comrades will come back for anything you can't manage. That's all for today.'

'Are you asking us to loot the homes of civilians, like the Germans do?' asked William.

'Those are the orders. And questions aren't welcome,' retorted Foster as he went on to assign other tasks, calculating that he wouldn't get through them all until evening.

That night, William couldn't sleep, despite the soft patter of rain on the roof. For hours he listened to soldiers snoring, or tossing and turning in their bunks. Then he went outside and looked for the stars. The rain soaked his face. The sky was puffy and dark, like an omen; of what, he could not say.

At dawn, he was the first to go outside, and he waited for Martin in the forecourt. He took from his rucksack the chocolate bar he was supposed to keep for emergencies. He ate half of it and put away the rest. He clutched his rifle tightly. It was very calm at that early hour; he didn't even feel as if he was at war. He turned his wrist to look at his watch. A sharp crack ran over the dial. It had stopped at 10.27 in the morning, long before he left for Ypres.

When William was a boy, he would wait for the clock to reach the late afternoon, the time his mother put down her needle, thread and dressmaker's tape measure, and they would go out for a walk. Usually, they would walk around the city, occasionally ending up in a place William did not know. A street, a square or a park. His mother liked the idea of showing him new areas, and she, too, was discovering many for the first time. One day they found themselves in front of a house. The walls were crumbling, windows were missing here and there, and the door was hanging off its hinges. It looked as if it had been abandoned for many years.

'If you feel brave enough, we can go in and have a look. What do you say, Will? Are you up for an adventure?'

'D'you already know what's in there, Mum?'

'I have no idea. That's why we should find out.'

'What if we find something bad?'

'It's just an abandoned house, Will. But if we do, then we'll face it together.'

*

'Where are you from, Edgar?'

'The North. You?'

'West.'

'A rifleman, then?'

'Yes.'

'That makes two of us.'

'Here, d'you have any idea what exactly we're supposed to be looking for here?'

'Something useful, but I don't even think Foster and the major know *exactly* what.'

'I got that feeling.'

'Anyway, it's not a difficult task. Before we do anything, let's find the place they marked out on the map.'

'What if someone's waiting for us there?'

'Someone who, William? The Germans are at the front.'

'Someone hostile, then.'

'Then I guess we'll have to figure out their intentions.'

'And how do we do that?'

'The best thing to do is to shoot him before he shoots us. We're at war, Turner, and the war doesn't ask questions. We shouldn't either.'

'Edgar.'

'Yes?'

'Why did you join up?'

'I've got a place to sleep here, food to eat. People to talk to.'

'What about your family?'

'I don't have anyone left. It's been like that for a very long time.'

William was about to reply 'Me, too,' but then he thought of his father and imagined him in the workshop, hunched over his bench. Even though they hardly spoke, at least he was still alive.

'What did you do before, Edgar?'

'I unloaded drink crates and took them to pubs. I'm small but strong. But I wasn't working enough to afford myself two decent meals a day. I was hungry, William. I'm already thirty. There's no place for someone like me in that world. If I'm good in battle and stand out, maybe they'll give me a job in the army. That's why I joined up. What about you?'

'I made a promise.'

'A promise?'

William was about to say more, but Martin yanked his coat hard.

'Hey, let's hide behind that bush.'

'Where?'

'Follow me,' Martin said and ran to crouch behind the bush, pointing his rifle. 'There are people down there. They might even be soldiers.'

In the distance, a long line of men, women and children were walking along the road in William and Martin's direction. Some were pulling small carts behind them, others baskets. Most of them were just dragging themselves along.

As they came closer, William noticed that their heads were bowed.

'Where are they going?'

'Away from Ypres. But I don't think they know exactly where either,' Martin replied, lowering his rifle.

William pictured their bombarded homes and imagined that the long line of human beings was composed of families, or individuals, who had not known one another until a few weeks or just days ago. Perhaps they had greeted one another with a certain cordiality at the baker's, or the post office. Or shared a nod before returning to the

18

routines that marked their daily lives – working until late, dinner, a fleeting caress before sleep – certain that the next day would be the same as the last. They were as assured of this as they were of the arrival of summer or Christmas Day, and this conviction would have lasted all the way up until one precise moment. A moment which was a sound: the sound of war, which brought with it a shared knowledge that they could no longer stay where they were, and the hope of saving something – clothes, objects and, most importantly, their lives.

When William left for the war, he imagined divisions of soldiers fighting against each other to conquer a piece of land and take the front a little further forward until victory or defeat; he seldom thought of those who had not chosen war.

He felt as if he was watching an intimate, endless church service. An hour passed before the last evacuees faded from view into dots on the horizon. Martin tapped William on the shoulder. 'We can go now.'

They came off the path and walked through the scrub, occasionally ducking behind trees to make sure no one was waiting in ambush for them. They held their rifles out in front, as they had been taught during training.

They stopped in a clearing, under the rainy leaves of chestnut trees, and, in silence, shared some bread and butter. Martin nibbled at his food; William ate quickly. He took his camera out of his rucksack as soon as he had finished, framing Martin, who was leaning against a tree and the smudge of his surroundings, all grey.

When William took photos, he would position his subject within their environment so that, once developed, the image would stay fixed in a precise memory. William thought that one's memory of people came from fixing them in a precise time and place; that's how his mind worked.

He waited for his comrade to bring his food to his mouth and pressed down on the shutter.

'What d'you do that for?' Martin asked.

'I try to keep memories.'

'Often memories hurt, then they fade sooner or later. Better not to have them, William.'

After their rest the young men kept going, trudging over the muddy ground until the brushwood and trees subsided and they could make out a couple of houses and a stable block in the distance. The land, which must have once held crops, was struggling to rise above the water. William recalled the sluices on the Yser river, opened by the tiny Cogge and mighty Geeraert. His boot sank into the mud, almost up to his knee. He dipped in a finger and brought it to his mouth.

'It's salty.'

'Come on, let's go,' Martin said.

The houses were simple, built for families of four or five, on a hill that was just high enough to keep them free of the water. Martin placed his rucksack on the edge of a pit next to the remnants of an abandoned horse fence and took out the map.

'Here we are.'

'Now what?'

'We start the search. You go to that house – I'll go to the other.'

'Fine.'

'William?'

'Yes?'

'If you see someone, don't think. Shoot.'

'I won't think, I'll shoot. Good luck, Private Martin.'

'Same to you, Private Turner.'

*

William found the door of the house ajar, as if the owners had left in a rush. Maybe something had driven them out with their animals. The arrival of the North Sea, he thought, or some bit of the war that had reached those parts for some unknown reason.

He carefully scrutinised every corner of the small hall; the only piece of furniture was a wooden bench. The floorboards were waterlogged; a shoehorn was nailed to the wall. Nothing suggested that someone might be there. He took off his drenched hat and woollen coat and placed them carefully on the bench. He was cold, but he would definitely fall ill if he kept his sodden clothes on.

There wasn't much to pillage from the house. Some chairs, a cupboard, a wooden table. There were a few crumbs on the table; who knew how long they had been there? He opened the cupboard and found a jar of rotten jam on the bottom shelf.

In the next-door room there were three beds, one big and two small, the covers thrown back. The scene suddenly made him sad, and he tried to swallow the emotion, but he couldn't quite manage it. He was reminded of the room in which his father and mother slept. When he was a child, he would go in on Sunday mornings as soon as he woke up. He had stopped doing this once he turned eight, and the memory had faded during his adolescence, resurfacing now for the first time.

It was time to go back and he was empty-handed.

As William neared the hallway, he heard a faint noise. He held his breath. Nerves of steel, he told himself, tightly gripping his rifle.

He tried in vain to control his heartbeat. Perhaps it was his imagination, or at most a scurrying mouse. If there was one thing he really disliked, it was mice.

One thing was certain: there was nothing in this house. He and Martin had walked for hours in vain. He picked up his soaked coat and hat and was making to leave when he heard the noise again.

Clutching his Lee–Enfield with all his might, William turned around and went back inside. He checked the rooms. Nothing. He sat down on a chair. Inhaled, exhaled for a long time. He heard the noise again, and another noise – a vibration, coming from above. He looked up. He could just make out the outlines of an opening in the ceiling.

He must stay calm; he could do this. He would climb up and act like a real soldier.

Standing on a chair, he took hold of the trapdoor, which squeaked open. He smelled mould; this must have been where they stored their cured meat. There was a retractable ladder. He pulled it down and climbed the steps slowly. He was frightened, but his duty as a soldier urged him on.

The attic was quite big, at least as big as the room below, poorly lit by the light filtering in through the trapdoor. Keeping his rifle pointed, he waited for his eyes to adjust to the darkness.

'Is anyone there?' he asked. He propelled himself forwards to the other side of the attic; empty crates and a rotten wooden cupboard were strewn around the floor.

'Come out,' he said.

He grasped the doorknob of the cupboard, ready to shoot, as he'd been trained to, as Martin had told him, and opened the door.

A young girl was crouching inside. She was holding an unlit candle in one trembling hand and covering her face with the other.

'Get up,' he ordered.

She did not move.

William stood there, pointing his rifle, unsure what to do next. Finally she raised her head. Her long hair was tousled and her face dirty, as if she had fallen into a pile of ashes. He looked into her eyes.

He could not tell what colour they were in the half-light, but he saw something in them, and if anyone had asked him he would have sworn it was a request.

'Get up,' he whispered to her.

The girl continued to look at him.

'D'you speak my language?'

Silence.

Then he lowered his weapon, going against Martin's advice and everything they had taught him in training.

William reached out his hand. She waited, as if to make sure that he meant her no harm, then took it, giving it a light squeeze. He led her across the attic in the half-light and helped her down the ladder. When they reached the bottom, she put down the candle and sat in a chair.

'Is this where you live?' He gestured to their surroundings.

The girl followed his finger with her gaze, then shook her head.

'Where are you from?'

Silence.

'Are you from these parts?'

No answer.

They had not given him instructions about what to do in this kind of situation. He took her arm to help her stand, but she wriggled out of his grip, shaking her head. William realised she had a wound on her elbow, and he released her.

'I don't want to hurt you.'

Silence.

'I'm going to put my rifle on the ground now. There. Is that all right? Yes?'

The girl stared at him fearfully. She must have been very familiar with weapons, at least since the Germans had arrived in Ypres.

William suddenly noticed the colour of her eyes. A deep blue, like the North Sea. He looked at her face. Though dirty and tired, her features were as delicate as waves resting momentarily on sand. He noticed a sensation in the pit of his stomach that he had never felt before, that he would only understand later – the desire to stay with her. He put his rucksack on the floor and took out the remaining piece of chocolate. The girl took it, unwrapped it, and greedily shoved it in her mouth.

Then, once she seemed calmer, he rummaged around for some gauze in his small first-aid bag. He wrapped it around her arm, trying not to squeeze it too tightly. She stood looking at him the whole time without saying a word. Little by little, the fear in her eyes dissipated.

'Is that better?' he asked.

The girl did not answer.

He opened the map and placed it next to her.

'We are here,' he said. 'Where are you from?'

The girl craned her neck to look at the map, trying to work it out. She pointed at a place.

'Ypres?'

She nodded.

'Were you with the people who were leaving?'

With two fingers he mimicked footsteps and pointed in the direction of the path.

The girl nodded.

'Why did you come here?'

She looked at him for a long time. She must have been a few years younger than him – fifteen, sixteen? Then she pointed back to the place on the map.

'I understand that you're from Ypres.'

She continued to hold her finger there.

William pointed to where he'd seen all of those people walking a few hours earlier. The girl shook her head.

'Don't you want to leave? Listen, it's not safe for you here, more soldiers might come. There's a place not far from here,' he said and he pointed with his finger, 'a forest near Ypres. From what I hear, the war hasn't arrived there yet.'

'Ploegsteert,' said the girl.

'Yes, near Ploegsteert. Wait.'

William opened his notebook, flicking to the page on which he had listed all of his equipment. He went

25

through it carefully and drew a firm line through some
of the entries:

~~one package~~
~~emergency tin of meat, two emergency tins of biscuits,~~
~~two emergency tins of peas, an emergency chocolate~~
~~bar, first-aid medication~~

'Here, these should tide you over for a while at least,' he
said, and placed the tins, packet of biscuits and medication
next to her.

The girl inadvertently brushed the back of his hand as
she took them and rested it there for a moment.

'What's your name?' He tapped his own chest. 'William
Turner, Private.'

'William,' said the girl.

'And you?'

The girl hesitated.

'Wait, I want to take a photograph of you.'

Now, for the first time in his life, William was no longer
interested in the setting surrounding his subject; he just
wanted to photograph her. She folded her arms and he leaned
forward. It looked as if there were waves in the middle of
her eyes. They were calm and sad eyes, like the sea when
the sun has almost set, when there's no longer anyone
watching it; similar to William's own eyes. Despite his young
age, he had always felt as if he noticed beautiful things when
it was already too late.

'Have you ever been here?' he asked, showing her the
North Sea on the map.

The girl shook her head.

'When all this is over, I could take you there,' he said, pointing first to her, then to himself, mimicking with two fingers the steps that would lead them to the deep blue on the coloured map.

The girl nodded. She came closer and, without warning, silently placed her lips on William's cheek, immediately drawing back. He swore he could see the foam of the waves on the room's wet floorboards. He would later recount this sudden kiss: 'It seemed like the sea was everywhere.'

'Hey! Turner.' He heard a loud call from the yard.

'Private Turner, are you all right?'

Martin.

'I'm here, I'm coming,' he shouted out. Then he turned to the girl. 'I have to go, otherwise he'll come looking for me and find you. He might want to take you to the camp, and that's not a good place for you,' he told her, pointing to the exit.

She nodded.

'The map – keep it.'

'Ploegsteert,' she said.

'Yes, Ploegsteert.'

William secured his rucksack and slung it over his shoulder. He picked up his rifle, walked across the hall and out into the afternoon light, where the rain was driving down. Martin was waiting for him. But William was thinking about the girl.

About the girl and the sea.

Martin was holding a crate in his hands. 'I found some wine, William! What about you?'

*

Someone had retrieved some woollen blankets. The returning soldiers sat wrapped in them, soaked, as they waited for their supper. A fire had been lit under the canopies, and one soldier had found some dried meat and old bread. Another two arrived with a tin of oil.

The cook, who they called Al – just Al – gestured to the soldiers to bring everything into the pantry. Then he went back to tending to his Great Bean Soup, a delicacy the soldiers excitedly anticipated, as if it was a blessing from the heavens, made even holier on earth by Father Adams. He repeatedly blessed the pots with the sign of the cross, hoping that this benevolent outpouring of Christian spirit would yield something in return as soon as the soup was ready; a bigger portion of food, perhaps.

The supplies had arrived at the command post in the afternoon. Al had cleverly divided and stored the goods so that there would be enough in the days to come. It was Great Bean Soup day when the everyday slop – water, broad beans, potatoes, turnips, a handful of meat or lard, scraps of salvaged stock, all tossed haphazardly into the pots – was enhanced with large quantities of beans.

When Martin had delivered the bottles of wine, he sensed they would end up in Major Weasel's personal store. So, he had kept a bottle for himself and William, who was now sitting, shivering in front of the fire.

'Have a sip, it'll help,' said Martin as he dunked his bread into the Great Bean Soup. William took a gulp of wine and immediately felt better.

'What if someone tells the major?'

'They're all busy, look.'

A few soldiers were talking among themselves, but most of them were focused hard on eating, like the two of them, or writing.

'What are they writing?' William asked.

'Who knows, kid? I've never written anything in my life. I'm not very good with words. I only know how to sign my name on documents. Maybe they want to let their loved ones know they're all right.'

William took another sip. He looked at his watch, frozen at 10.27 in the morning. He would fix it, he thought, in his father's workshop, as soon as he returned home. He imagined his father now, still working, even though it was dark. He could send him a postcard, tell him that he was all right, that soon he would be sent to the front, to defend the front line and to fight. He would also like to explain the reason for his departure to his father, but then he realised that postcards don't have enough room for all those words and that the blank sheets used for letters had too much space.

He stood up, bottle in hand, three-quarters full.

It was still raining.

The rain drummed on the canopies and bounced off Reagan's postcard. He had been a barber's apprentice, and William offered him a sip of wine as he read over what Reagan had written.

Mother, it read, *I'm waiting to leave for the front. The days aren't so tiring so far. They feed us quite well and we have a sheltered place to sleep. They put me in charge of cutting the new recruits' hair. I've only just arrived, and I don't know how long I'll stay, but I want to reassure you now: when the war is over, we'll spend an afternoon together, just you and me. I'll give you a wonderful haircut, not like the ones I rush through here all day long. I'll take you to drink tea and we'll eat biscuits, like ladies and gentlemen do. Wait for me and pray for me,*

Yours,
Jul

The raindrops bounced off Kutcher's postcard; he was a former domestic servant who now worked in the pantry and distributed the rations with Al. He was writing, too.

You were right, winter is coming and it's cold; but to tell you the truth, the whole truth. . .

The raindrops bounced off Ericson's postcard. He was a student of something or other; no one could remember what. He shook his pen; it had stopped working.

If you can put more bacon and cigarettes in the parcel you send me at Christmas . . . Oh, and a razor, don't forget the razor. Today I borrowed one from Reagan, the barber . . . In the meantime, when we get to the front, I'll rely on his generosity and that of my comrades to share theirs with me . . . They say that the war is coming to an end and that one way or another we'll all be home by the New Year. That's also why I want

*the razor, so I can come home looking neat and tidy.
I often think about the house we must fix up so we
can live there after we . . .*

And on Tyler's postcard. He was one of the stretcher-bearers, a taciturn fellow who had gone backwards
and forwards from the front line to the third line more
than anyone else. He'd been there since the beginning
of the war. He ate alone in a corner and hoped to go
home soon.

*Dear Mum, dear Dad, I miss you. After what I've seen
with my own eyes at the front, I can say with absolute
certainty that the newspaper reports aren't entirely . . .*

As soon as Tyler saw William leaning over him, he laid a
hand over his postcard and grabbed the bottle, knocking
back some wine, wiping his mouth with the sleeve of his
coat before handing it back.

'What d'you see at the front?'

'You can see for yourself,' Tyler said, pointing to the
field hospital.

'I don't think I'm allowed to enter.'

'At night there's only one guard. Peek in and you'll
realise that you'd better shoot well and hang around.'

'For what?'

'For a German to shoot faster than you.'

William crossed the forecourt to return to the dormitory. As
he walked, he kept his eyes fixed on the field hospital – where

the severely wounded were housed. He brushed his lips with two fingers and thought about the girl with the mini North Sea in her eyes, the girl he had kept quiet about, to keep her safe, who had kissed him so suddenly. He had never been kissed before.

He felt he must find her again, stay with her. He would keep the promise he had made to his mother, and as soon as the war was over, he would look for the girl. Together, they would walk all the way to the sea.

Lost in thought, William bumped into Father Adams, who was sitting on a stool, greedily drinking beer from his mug. His vestments, an aspergillum for sprinkling holy water and a jug lay at his feet. He was writing in a leather-bound diary; there was a badly drawn cross in black ink on the title page.

'Padre, would you like the last sip?' William asked, handing him the bottle of wine.

'Where did that come from? Ah, best not to know,' Adams said, taking it from William and polishing it off in one gulp.

'Are you writing to someone, too?'

'I'm working on new prayers. What's troubling you, young man?'

'I'm not troubled.'

'If there's one thing any parish priest knows how to do, it's to recognise when others are upset. You can see it in the eyes.'

'In the eyes?'

'You're looking down.'

William remained silent.

'Well?' Father Adams pressed him.

'Today I saw hordes of people walking away from their homes. I wonder if they'll ever return.'

'If it's the good Lord's will.'

'And d'you know? What God wants, I mean.'

'Oh, I have no idea at this point. If I knew, maybe I wouldn't be here.'

'What d'you mean?'

'I'm just trying to do my bit while I wait for the good Lord to make a decision about ending the war.'

'Out there on the front . . . It's quite a situation, isn't it?'

'Nasty.'

'Padre?'

'Yes?'

'You've seen it in person, haven't you?'

'The front?'

'Yes.'

'I've only been once, in October, to comfort the soldiers before you. They told me we had organised the attack in great detail, and it didn't go well, son. But I trust that the good Lord will soon intervene on our behalf, since we're on the right side. You must be wondering what it's like, out there at the front.'

'Exactly.'

Father Adams looked up at the sky.

'Stormy and dark, like this weather.'

'Father Adams . . . Padre.' It was Foster's voice; he appeared behind William and stood between the two of them. 'The two soldiers held in confinement have been asking for you.'

'Never any peace for the parish priest.' Adams huffed as he placed his diary on the ground and heaved himself up. 'I'm coming,' he said, and to William, 'We'll have to finish our conversation another time.'

Who were the men who'd ended up in confinement? Even if William had known their names, they wouldn't have meant much to him. There were too many of them, hundreds of boys who didn't know one another, united by the colour of their uniform, by the same fragile sense of belonging: it was a thin thread running between them, like the one his mother used to put through the eye of the needle to mend clothes. We are born, William thought, longing for a thread, at least one thread, that binds us to others, and stops us from getting lost in the emptiness of the world, and we end up carrying this desire throughout all of our lives.

William stood on the semi-deserted forecourt, which was now dimly lit by the fires, watching the rain fall against the flickering light. He reflected on the rain; how it was composed of thousands of tiny drops falling in the same direction, like marching soldiers. They might have looked like a single mass to the distracted observer, but each drop was single and unique.

*

William waited until the guard stationed at the entrance of the field hospital put down his rifle and went to take a long, satisfying pee.

He opened the door quietly, just wide enough to squeeze through, but it still made a noise. Why hasn't anyone thought of oiling these hinges? he wondered as he slipped inside.

A faint light filtered into the room; he could just make out the first beds. But as the door shut behind him it went completely dark. William guessed that the guard had resumed his post. He imagined him, his breeches around his ankles, dashing back to the hospital as soon as he heard the door creak.

The image made him smile in the darkness. Then he heard a moan towards the back of the room, which was soon joined by another, slightly louder, and then another. Then the room fell into a deep silence. A minute passed, and he heard a fourth moan, closer this time.

He listened to the brief symphony of guttural sounds, imperceptible to anyone outside this room. They were the whispers of those who no longer had the strength to speak of their pain. Inside the hospital there were soldiers who had been badly wounded by the bayonets and gunfire, maimed by grenades, or God knows what – soldiers who had been recruits before they fought at the front; and before that they were recruits, boys, just like William.

He now understood why only doctors and officers were allowed into the hospital, why it was guarded at all hours of the day and night. The hospital contained the secret of the front line: the truth of what it did to the men who fought there.

A beam of light suddenly flashed behind William, casting his shadow forward. He turned around.

It was Major Weasel and the guard. The guard was pointing his rifle at William.

'What are you doing here?' the major demanded.

35

William tried to answer, but saliva clogged his throat. He swallowed and tried to say, 'I just wanted to have a look.'

'You're in trouble, boy, you know that?'

'Yes,' he replied.

'You'd better give me a reasonable answer. What are you doing here?'

'I wanted to know what the front does to people.'

'What's your name?'

'William Turner. Private.'

'Private Turner, go and rest. Because tomorrow we'll make the announcement – at sunset you'll cross the third and second line.'

'Major Weasel . . .'

'You must answer "Yes, Sir."'

'Yes, sir, Major Weasel.'

'You must answer "Yes, sir, Major Weasel, it is my honour to serve my country on the front line."'

'Yes, sir, Major Weasel, it is my honour to serve my country on the front line.'

'Good. And make sure you make yourself useful when you're there. Or you'll end up like the two in confinement, who tried to run away.'

'What will happen to them?'

'They'll be executed soon,' said Major Weasel, motioning the guard to lower his rifle.

William undressed in the darkness of the dormitory, rummaging in his rucksack for dry clothing.

He would have to find Martin and tell him they were leaving for the front line the next day, but he didn't want to risk waking the other soldiers or attracting the attention of the guards patrolling the yard.

William huddled under his blanket, shivering. Little by little, fatigue caught up with him and he fell asleep. He dreamed of his mother.

*

'Will,' his mother says.

She has light hair; her skin is pale and reminiscent of a late summer evening, when the air begins to cool, and the outline of the moon and its dark smudges emerge in the clear sky.

His mother's skin is fragrant. Sometimes William wonders if everyone can smell it, or if it's just him because he's her son. His schoolmates also say that their mothers' skin smells good. They once all tried to describe it, each in their own way, but it didn't work, because a good smell is not made of words, it simply enters the nostrils. One day after school, someone suggested lining up all of their mothers and smelling them, but William didn't think this was a good idea. Even though he was only eight years old, he understood quite well that the same smell can be entirely different to two different noses. He knew this because many of his classmates liked the smell of stewed beans, or peas, and he didn't. Besides, he didn't like the idea of his mother being sniffed at by all those noses. Especially Guy's and Marcus's, who sniffled unpleasantly even when they didn't have a cold.

'Will, are you listening to me?'

His mother pulls him close, and he realises that he is walking in the middle of the road and that he is in danger of being run over.

'Will, my darling, d'you want them to turn you into scrambled eggs?'

'Mhm,' he grumbles.

Everyone likes scrambled eggs, especially with bacon on the weekends or special days. But Will is not bothered about them. To be honest, he's not that bothered about food in general. He eats when his stomach rumbles or when his parents demand it. With very few exceptions.

He even made a list once; his father asked him to. 'Concentrate hard and write down all the foods you really like, so that we can try and give them to you. When we get the chance, that is.'

His father gave him a notebook and a pencil. On the first page, it read: *A list of things I really like to eat.* It was a good start.

He spent three days working on the list; he had to have a good think. On the first day, he added a few things, but come the evening, he rubbed them out, no longer sure that he liked them. The second day all he wrote was: *ham*. Oh, he does like ham, he goes mad for it, but they rarely have it at home, maybe because they can't afford it.

By the evening of the third day, his list was ready. He looked it over many times. It wasn't long but he was satisfied.

Ham, chocolate, cucumber, ham, pudding, milk, potatoes, chocolate.

He realised that he had written *ham* and *chocolate* twice. If his teacher read the list she would surely correct him, but he thinks that it was important to write them twice, because he likes them exactly twice as much as the other things.

And he's on the road that afternoon, because his mother is taking him to a bakery. They had started out late and he was anxious. He tried to get her to hurry up; if they weren't quick the shop would close, but his mother, a seamstress, had to finish a dress that was being delivered the next day. He is walking on the road because the pavement is busy with people who can slow you down when you're in a hurry. Anyway, he's an alert child and would easily hear a carriage approaching.

We will get there before it closes, keep saying it, Will, and it'll be true, we will get there before it closes.

Except that it closes in ten minutes. His mother takes his hand and he can no longer overtake the people on the pavement by walking in the road. She is wearing a beautiful watch on her wrist. It's valuable, too. God, he can't tell if it's really valuable, but he remembers when his father came home a few days earlier and put a package on the table. His mother opened it and brought her hand to her mouth. William has learned that when his mother sees something that makes her happy, she brings her hand to her mouth. And after a while she smiles. The smile that followed as soon as she tried on that watch left little doubt: she was happy. His father told her how he had found it at a flea market and bought it for a good price, because of the poor state it was in. But now that he had restored it, it had acquired a certain value.

It's not just that they have ten minutes before the bakery closes, but it will take them at least double that time to get there.

They are moving at a brisk pace, however, and anyway, according to William's calculations, if they don't encounter too many acquaintances, they could make up time, especially considering that Mr Ford, the owner of the bakery, sometimes stays a little longer to set up the shop window for the next day.

'Good morning, ma'am,' William hears when they are close to the large crossroads that leads to the bakery which is just opposite.

'Good morning to you, Dorothy. How are you?' William's mother replies, slowing to a standstill.

Dorothy Parker. DOROTHY PARKER! William breaks out in a cold sweat. Of all his mother's clients, Dorothy Parker is the most chatty. In fact, she is the chattiest person he has ever met in his entire eight-year-old life. Once she starts talking, Dorothy Parker never stops. She begins the conversation with comments about the weather and continues with household chores, offering advice that nobody wants. DOROTHY PARKER. William closes his eyes and makes a wish: Dorothy Parker is in a hurry, repeat it-Will-then-it-will-be-true. Dorothy Parker is in a mad rush and will say goodbye to your mother.

'I'll be bringing you that party dress that you mended for me two years ago,' William hears her say, and at that moment he wishes he had the power to make people just disappear.

'Is there something wrong with it?'

'It'll have to be widened a little . . .'

William tries to pull on his mother's skirt, but she waves him off. He knows that there is not much money in his family, and that his mother always says that every client is to be treated with kid gloves, because, if they sense any disrespect, they will choose another seamstress in an instant.

William concentrates – he even closes his eyes – but when he opens them, Dorothy Parker is still there. He looks at the time on his mother's watch. It's three minutes to closing time; but maybe a few more if Mr Ford is running late.

He turns towards the crossroads. If they continued along the pavement they would never make it in time, even if Dorothy Parker was to disappear right that moment. Crossing the road is the only solution, William thinks. Take a deep breath and run as fast as you can, then keep running towards the bakery, arrive before Mr Ford closes and ask for your favourite chocolate cake, explaining that your mother stopped to talk to Dorothy Parker. Everyone in the neighbourhood knows her, and Mr Ford would understand. William will tell Mr Ford that his mother will come back and settle the bill the next day.

When William's mother turns to her son, she can't find him. 'Will?' she calls. 'Will?' Her gaze moves along the pavement and then stops at the crossroads, where she sees her son in the middle of the road, motionless between two carriages, unable to go forward or back. He is gripped by a fear that she can feel, even from a distance.

Without a moment's thought, she throws herself headlong into the road, dodges one carriage, then another. She lets go of her bulky handbag so she can run towards William unencumbered.

*

William woke up at first light. He pulled on his jumper; his coat was still wet with rain from the day before. He scanned the sky from the doorway; it was swollen and grey. Still raining. He hoped it would stop soon before he left for the front.

He thought of his father in his workshop, bent over the laden workbench.

When William was beside him, he would count his wrinkles; he had too many for his age. His father's life had stopped eleven years earlier, when William crossed the road to Mr Ford's bakery. He remembered when the doctor came out of his parents' bedroom, beckoning them in; his mother lay motionless on the bed, staring up at the ceiling. Most of all, he remembered the silence: her involuntary silence, and his father's insistent silence. The way he stared at the wall, choosing not to speak, because any words that came out of his mouth would be words of blame for his son. William's silence, the silence of a boy who has discovered guilt too soon. A viscous substance which slithers down your throat and clogs your heart, your lungs, your stomach.

For the last eleven years, William's father had been fighting a war; his enemy was time and it flowed mercilessly. Second by second, minute by minute. First, William's father would have liked to have stopped time, then turned it back. Perhaps one day he would succeed. Who better than him – he who knew the secrets of time: he had made a job out of it, repairing watches. And he was good.

William could not fight his father's war, so he would fight the one he had chosen for himself. The sooner this war – *my* war – ends, the more people I'll be able to save, he thought. He would soon return, find the girl with the North Sea in her eyes, and perhaps reinvent his life with her.

There were no major announcements before they left for the front. Foster called them all together, with Major Weasel at his side. 'It's time,' was all he said.

That morning, soldiers bustled about packing their rucksacks, making their beds and returning their blankets, which would be folded and distributed to the new recruits and the severely wounded returning from the front. They were served a double portion of beef, sausage and bread, with cigarettes, beer, and a few tins of meat, and told that on the front line they would regularly receive rum to combat the cold. They sang together as they ate and it gave them strength. It felt so much like a party that their fears evaporated.

Everyone kept saying that the war would be over by Christmas: that they would witness – and take part in – a great victory. William felt invigorated. The shadows haunting him earlier were now distant echoes. He took his camera out of his rucksack and snapped a few photos: of Martin, Foster and groups of other soldiers, who immediately posed, smiling. He promised to send them copies once the war was over, and filled his notebook with their home addresses.

When it was time to leave, their bellies were so full and their morale so high the soldiers felt like students on a field trip. They hugged each other, joked around, preparing themselves for the journey ahead. They set off at sunset, marching forth to change the world.

It was 5 December, 1914.

TWO

Flanders, 1933

'I'M SO HUNGRY,' SAID the boy, looking up at the sky.
'D'you think it'll rain?'

The man tried to read the sky, the clouds rapidly moving
and changing.

'I hope not. It's pretty windy, but I think the clouds will
lift as quickly as they came in. Are you cold?'

The boy pulled up the collar of his coat. 'A little, but
I'll be all right. I've got two jumpers on.'

'True.'

'Dad, what d'you have in your bag?'

'Just some clothes. We'll be glad of them if the temperature drops again.'

'We left in such a hurry, Mum seemed worried.'

'We were going to miss the train.'

'Why didn't she come with us?'

'She had important things to do, but I'm sure she's
looking forward to seeing us now.'

The man handed the boy a sandwich; he took a bite,
chewed and swallowed.

'That thing about the rain making the North Sea . . .
Did William Turner tell you that?' he asked.

'Yes.'

'And d'you think it's true?'

The man brushed a crumb off his cheek.

'I don't know, maybe. I like to think so.'

'When we get home, I'd like to ask about it at school,' the boy said.

The man's face darkened. He thought of the word *home*, the familiar feeling it aroused in himself and his family. Before he had left the house with his son, he had stood looking at the wooden table around which they shared all their meals. They had bought it from a carpenter, years before. It was this image that came to mind when he thought of his family: the three of them in the house, sitting around the table eating dinner. His wife had quietly said to him, 'Go.' Then she had stroked her son's head as he rubbed his sleepy eyes. 'It'll be a wonderful adventure, you'll see.'

'D'you like school?' the man asked the boy.

'Sometimes I do and sometimes I don't,' he said, fiddling with a button on his jacket. 'Let's just say I do. All my friends are at school. And sometimes they even teach us something interesting.'

'And when don't you like it?'

'When I have to study too much. They should give us less homework.'

'Well, when you get back, your teachers will answer all your questions about the rain and the sea.'

The boy put the last piece of his sandwich into his still-hungry mouth.

'Better now?' asked his father.

'Better. It's not nice being hungry when you don't have anything to eat.'

'What d'you mean?'

'I was thinking about what you told me about Martin – that he could only eat once a day. Some of my schoolmates are like that, too. That's why he went to war, isn't it? Because he was hungry?'

'I think so. And because he believed in what he was doing. He believed it with all his heart. It's sad to say, but he did.'

'Why d'you say it's sad?'

'You see, when you fear for your life and think that it's other people's fault, you no longer see them as people, but as enemies. Maybe Martin made this mistake. Many people have, I'm afraid.'

'You, too?'

'Me, too, at first.'

'But why?'

'I was young and believed what I was told. By the time I realised how wrong I was it was too late for me to turn back.'

'What about William Turner? Did he think so, too?'

'He set out to settle a score with his past. He didn't know how wrong he was. The only way forward, young man, is the present.'

The man recalled the previous spring, a day when he and his son were walking along the street in their small town near Munich. As they turned the corner, they had seen a mass of people, many of them students, crowded around a large fire blazing in the centre of the square. The man had thought a fire had broken out, that these people were rushing about to put it out. As he approached, and to his amazement, he saw the students were actually stoking the fire – with books. He had called a nearby policeman, who was standing very still with his hands behind his back.

'Why aren't you stopping them?' he had asked, pointing to the fire.

'Everything looks fine,' the policeman had replied. 'Behave like a good German and you've nothing to fear.'

The man and his son had stayed there for a long time, watching the books burn. It was then, as he watched the fire, that it occurred to him he must do something. After so many years, William Turner's words about choosing one's path echoed in his mind.

The boy had tugged at his father's jacket. 'Why are they doing this?' he had asked, but his father didn't have an answer to give him.

He had asked himself the same question, many years before, when he was in the trenches fighting against the British: 'Why are we doing this?' Even then he didn't have an answer.

'The only path we can take is the present, young man,' he repeated, as if to convince himself.

The boy looked down from the wall he was sitting on. He tried to imagine his father among the young soldiers.

'Dad, what did William Turner do after he marched through the trenches?'

'He learned that it's not fear that makes us weak.'

'What is it, then?'

'The refusal to understand who's standing in front of us.'

Flanders, 1914

THE SOLDIERS COULDN'T SLEEP that first night. Sergeant Blackwood Jones, a chubby man who oversaw military and logistical organisation on the front line, huffed and puffed as he ordered all new recruits to hurry up and clear out of the trenches.

The trenches were long expanses of zigzagging tunnels. Walls six feet long stood in front of them and behind them, on top of which were dozens of precariously stacked sandbags. Beyond these stood makeshift barbed wire lattices. The sandbags could hold off attacks, but not the shards of shrapnel which could mangle an arm or a leg, pierce a lung, crush a skull. They exploded into no man's land, the small strip of earth separating the allies from the German trenches. The shrapnel would whistle over the soldiers' heads on the front line, and most of it reached the second. If you didn't take cover, or if you leaned out to see what was happening in that plot of land separating the two armies, it was all over.

On that wounded earth of holes and craters were the mangled bodies of dead or dying soldiers whose nationality was only recognisable by the grey or khaki colour of their mud-spattered uniforms.

No one should end up in no man's land, not for anything in the world. William had understood this before he had even fired a shot. He also tried to understand how things worked in the trenches, as he cleared them of water, bucket in hand, cursing the rain he had so loved.

It poured down, the heavy drops pooling on the ground beneath him. The freezing mud almost reached his knees. William and the other soldiers filled their buckets with muddy water and tossed it over the barbed wire, trusting that a stray bullet or shrapnel wouldn't catch their arm – or, if it did, that the arm would not become infected before reaching the field hospital.

He felt that their movements were both necessary and senseless: the more they laboured to empty the trench, the more the mud rose up their legs. Haven't I done this my whole life? William asked himself. *Empty out mud.* The more that he'd filled buckets with memories, the more they'd piled up inside him, taking up all of the empty space.

William could barely stand up when dawn came, he was so exhausted. He put down the bucket. It continued to float in the mud before slowly sinking out of sight. Martin continued filling and emptying next to him, but despite his strength, he stopped when he saw other sleepy soldiers arriving to swap shifts.

The soldiers pointed in the direction of the dormitory. They walked, hunched over, to the second line and saw the sign: *The Good Pillow.*

They slipped into a large hole, dug several feet deep. It led to a large room whose walls were packed with straw. At the entrance, a reinforcement of sandbags held back some – but not all – of the rain. The water in the dorm rose right up to the edges of the mattresses, soaking them.

They lay down, exhausted, in the tight space, still in their coats. There were no blankets and no trace of the pillow the sign outside had promised.

They spent a few hours there, sleeping and waking continuously. Martin eventually got up to massage his sore neck. He made sure his comrade was awake.

'What a stupid name for a dormitory,' he said.

William turned away from him. He thought about the dream he had had before leaving for the front, the one featuring his mother. A dream that was a memory. *Emptying mud.* He looked at his watch.

How absurd, he thought. It had been eleven years since it had stopped, and he had promised himself that one day he would learn his father's trade and fix it. But his father had never taught him. He had merely given him delivery jobs, and William had never insisted on staying behind at the shop after closing time to learn its secrets. He had started helping his father with the deliveries when he was a boy, and that's what he did until the day he left for war: deliver the watches his father fixed. He was eight years old when his father had put him to work; when his mother's income stopped coming in.

William's father kept his eyes down while he wrapped up the watches. As a boy, William would attribute his father's behaviour to his shy character, but deep inside he knew that this was not the case. His father did not smile. Yet he used to smile, his thin lips just opening; he used to smile *before*. Before William crossed the road to get to Mr Ford's bakery on time and stopped in the middle of the crossroads. An eight-year-old boy stranded amid the bustle of horses and carriages, paralysed with fear, unable to move forward or back. Before his mother saw him – her son, caught in a flurry of traffic – and started running into the road, dropping her only handbag, which she never let go of when she went out. Before she threw her body between her son and a horse's hoof and fell to the ground, hitting her back, head and wrist – the wrist with the watch William's father had given her only a few days before.

When the doctor called them into the bedroom, his father had not been able to look at her. He had not even managed to look at William. His mother was still alive, but she wasn't speaking and could barely move. William had noticed that her watch was cracked, but it still worked, still ticked.

'We have to take her to a hospital so she can be treated,' the doctor had told them.

They had visited her once a week for several months. The treatment was expensive; his father had sold their small house to pay for it, and he and William had moved into the back of the shop. His mother had continued to live. And continued not to speak or move. All that time, William's father never stopped working. Even at night, his eyes were fixed on his workbench. They ate once a day, and William found neither chocolate nor ham on his plate. At the end of that year, a nurse called from the hospital to tell them she had passed away. Inside the envelope containing his mother's few personal belongings was her watch. William had taken it and put it on his wrist. He had done this in front of his father, who remained silent. As soon as he fastened it, he noticed that it had stopped at 10.27 in the morning. Who knows why it was stuck at that particular hour? Something inside must have broken, so that the slender hands no longer ticked round.

William woke up late in the morning, feeling a tickle at the bottom of his leg. He reached out his hand, his eyes still closed, and felt something strange.

A cotton ball, he thought, half asleep. No – something else, more like dog hair. It took him a few seconds to open his eyes and focus.

There was a mouse on his leg, a broken ID tag hanging from its mouth. It seemed to be staring at him.

William leaped away in fright, curling into himself. Terrified, the mouse abandoned the tag and scampered over the mattress.

'Have you just arrived?' asked the soldier who was lying a few cots away.

'Last night.'

'Take it easy, it's full of mice here. You'll get used to it.'

'Go away,' William half-whispered, so as not to wake the others. But the mouse stayed where it was.

William plucked up the courage to stretch out his foot and shove it off. The mouse jumped into the muddy water. William stayed completely still, trying to make sure it did not return.

Then he picked up the tag and read the name engraved on it: Julius. Did it belong to a soldier who slept in here? he asked himself.

Martin was already on his feet, his rifle on his shoulder.

'Our shift starts soon,' he said. 'It's time to show the Germans what we're made of. Stop playing with the mice and let's go.'

William took his rifle and followed Martin out of the dormitory into the trench.

*

Someone had managed to bring a huge pump to the front line to suck out the water. It worked, but it was not enough; the rain was too heavy. And there were not enough soldiers with buckets.

Soldiers without anything to do stood motionless, on the lookout for an attack from the Germans. It could come at any moment. A minute became an hour, an hour half a day, their feet soaking in the freezing water. The temperature had dropped by at least five degrees in the last few days. The soldiers' woollen coats and caps weren't much good in the cold.

By early afternoon, the soldiers could no longer feel their feet. They exchanged puffs of cigarettes with their lookout companions – a tiny movement, the only consolation in that long wait. Then a shot of rum and a few words, calling each other to attention. 'What was that noise?' They would clutch their rifles and hold their breath. 'You imagined it,' they would reply. They stamped their feet on the spot, feeling they might rot away if they didn't. 'Get ready! When the attack comes, we won't have much time,' they told one another, bolstering what strength they had. Meanwhile they looked ahead, behind, or sideways. And at the ground. Grey earth. Everywhere.

William started hoping that the Germans really would attack; then they could move. But there was only a desolate quiet beyond the trench, punctuated here and there by the drumming rain.

If a grenade doesn't kill us, the cold will, they all thought. But no one said it out loud: by now they had understood that despondency digs into the mind, that once it materialises into a word, it feeds fear. Fear which was already flourishing inside them all, like a fierce wild plant growing rampantly in a carefully tended garden.

It was not the fear of death – there had been no attack since they had entered the trenches – but rather, the impossibility of moving forwards or backwards, the restriction on moving freely around.

Their only freedom now was their view of the sky. It was the only thing that distinguished the trench from a grave. If the clouds had given way to sunshine, or at least a glimpse of blue, the soldiers might even have been able to imagine themselves up there, free.

'What the hell?' Martin said, pulling out what appeared to be a ball of dirt from his coat collar.

'Bloody lice,' said a soldier.

'I've already found two or three of them,' said Martin. 'There must be a nest of them somewhere.'

'Lice don't make nests,' the same soldier replied.

'Where do they come from?' asked William.

'They're everywhere. They'll end up devouring us, one bite at a time.'

'Hey, shut up, they're moving,' said Martin.

The sound of movement in the German trenches reached them from no man's land.

'What's going on?' asked William.

55

'They're preparing something. Get ready, I think we'll be leaving this mud soon.'

Martin volunteered to have a look, although his height did not allow him to rise much above the trench. William hoisted him aloft, just enough for him to see beyond the packed earth. The soldiers next to them remained silent, waiting for his signal.

'I can't see very well,' he said. 'It looks like there's movement . . . Men . . .'

'What are they doing?' William asked urgently.

'They're . . . Oh, these glasses. I need you to help me.'

Martin took them off and handed them to a soldier, who did his best to dry them with his uniform before returning them.

'There's too much rain to be certain of anything,' Martin said under his breath, as if the Germans could already hear him.

'Maybe we should call the sergeant,' said the soldier.

'I'll go and do it,' said another, crouching as he moved along the trench.

'Put me down, Turner.'

Martin landed feet first in the water. The neighbouring soldiers huddled around him for a few more details.

'I saw figures.'

'Above the trench?'

'It seemed so.'

'That's crazy.'

'The Germans are crazy. They say they're like animals – they don't care about dying, as long as they can kill even one of us.'

'That's right,' someone echoed.

'We should aim at their shadows and shoot.'

'Without the sergeant's orders?'

'Yes, without the sergeant's orders. By the time he arrives they'll have already gone back to their shelters.'

They put it to a vote. Waiting won. They had been waiting all day; shooting blindly hardly seemed like a good option to anyone. One mistake and they might start a crossfire. And what would they do then? They knew nothing about war tactics – certainly a lot less than Sergeant Blackwood Jones, who, after a good quarter of an hour, arrived holding a soggy bundle of paperwork under his arm.

'So?' he asked, muttering and smoothing his moustache.

Martin told him what he had seen.

'Private, you made me come all this way for shadows in the rain?'

'Maybe they weren't just shadows.'

'We decided to wait for you anyway,' William added.

'You did well. You, soldier with the glasses, what did you think you were doing? It's full of snipers out there. And you, go up and have a look,' the sergeant told William. 'We need confirmation to proceed.' William plucked up his courage and peeked out of the trench. He, too, seemed to see some movement on the enemy line; but it was vague, appearing and disappearing. Perhaps it was the wind blowing around the rain, shaping human figures. Or was it really the Germans preparing an attack? He could not tell.

Before ducking back down, he lowered his gaze, just long enough to see no man's land. The rain had filled the craters left by bombs; there were bodies everywhere.

One of them was still moving. The slow, pained actions of someone without any strength. William could not understand if he was calling for help, or simply waiting to die. The sound of the rain drowned out the soldier's dull voice. He could not understand whether the soldier was English or German, either, and he was unable to feel pity, if he was English, or satisfaction, if he was German. All he felt was a sense of powerlessness.

'Well?' asked Blackwood Jones.

'I can't tell.'

'Are they there or not?'

'Maybe . . .'

'Private, there are no maybes on the front line!'

'Common sense tells me they aren't. Who would prepare for an attack in the middle of this storm?'

'Ah, how little you know about war. And how little you know about Germans.'

The sergeant ordered a soldier to bring him a rubber cloth, which he hung over his head while he tried to flick through his papers; they were sodden, stuck together. He hesitated, smoothed his moustache, and looked ahead, in search of a solution, knowing that there was none. Soon it would be dark. Might the Germans attack as soon as night fell?

He organised the sentries among the machine guns slotted between the sandbags. If the Germans tried to approach them, they would be stopped by two hundred and fifty rounds a second. He felt satisfied with this decision, but then thought that it might not be enough just to defend themselves. They needed to make progress. Then it occurred to him that if that night passed without a hitch, he would have time to wait for the go-ahead from the commanders to organise his troops and take the Germans by surprise.

Many of the bodies lying in no man's land had been there for a few days; Sergeant Blackwood Jones had had the very same idea a short time before – to attack before being attacked. The only result had been fewer British soldiers to carry on fighting; but this time, he said to himself, it was different. The rain would turn from enemy to ally; it would cover them, and allow them to conquer the front line.

'Be ready for dawn. I'll report to headquarters and if they give me the go-ahead, I'll have more soldiers here. Tomorrow we'll show them what we're capable of.'

William felt his head spin. An ache in his back. Maybe it was a louse, maybe fear. They would be such easy targets, he thought.

'Is this the first time we're trying something like this?' he asked.

'In wind and heavy rain, yes, and that's why it's going to work,' said Blackwood Jones, smoothing his moustache with a confidence that immediately reassured the soldiers.

Later, morale waned, as the soldiers lay on their bunks in *The Good Pillow,* exchanging views and opinions, listening to William recount what he had seen out there in no man's land.

*

'Listen, soldier, I've seen this all before,'said a soldier William had never seen before. 'I've been here for more than a month. I'm a veteran now.' He had stubble on his chin and bore the acrid smell of someone who had not washed for a long time. 'It doesn't look good. They have bayonets and machine guns at the ready, just like us. The boy writhing in agony you saw in no man's land has been there for four days. I know because I was there when he fell. He was one of our comrades. And today he was still moving. How does he go on? Well, that's a mystery. I know what you're thinking, what all of you who have just arrived are thinking – why don't we go and save him? Because nobody has given us orders to. To go out there would mean getting skinned alive. A hundred of us would die to save one man. If we attack again tomorrow, many of us won't return.'

'Have you seen the Germans?' asked William. 'In the face, I mean.'

'Many of us fell by machine-gun fire, but many others came close to the enemy line. Like me. The Germans jumped out by the dozen, running fast like angry animals. I saw them, yes, but I couldn't tell you what one of them looked like. When you stand in front of an enemy soldier, you must keep only one thing in mind – that it's his life or yours.'

'We'll be faster than them,' said Martin.

'They're probably thinking the same thing in their muddy dormitories.'

'If Sergeant Blackwood Jones heard you, he'd give you a hard time.'

'D'you know what the sergeant did before he came here? He was an army clerk. A simple clerk. He knows nothing about war techniques, just like you and me, and I bet the German officers don't either, or the boys fighting.

Blackwood Jones reports on the situation and carries out orders, when he's not coming up with barmy ideas for headquarters to approve.'

'And you?' asked William. 'What did you do before? Why did you join up?'

'I was a professor. I studied Latin, Greek, Anglo-Saxon. If I get out of here alive, teaching literature is what I would like to do for the rest of my life. I couldn't tell you why I joined – not today, anyway. What I mean is that the story they spin about war is certainly much nobler than the war itself.' The soldier looked down, as if searching for more words in the dormitory's mud.

'Dry up,' another soldier shushed him. 'I say that tomorrow they'll find us ready for anything. We'll cross that strip of land and drive them back. By Christmas we'll have shut this all down.'

'Well said,' echoed Martin.

'Well said,' the others responded.

William realised that, in the general jubilation, the young professor was leaving the dormitory. He rose from his damp mattress and followed him. The professor lit his pipe on the threshold of the dugout and took a long, long puff.

'And you,?' he asked. 'How d'you end up here?'

'I made a promise,' said William.

'You promised to go to war?'

'I promised that as soon as I had the chance, I would save lives.' William paused. It had been right after his mother's funeral: he had placed a tulip on her grave and whispered that very promise to her.

'So you thought you would fight in the war?'

'Yes.'

'I'm sorry,' said the young professor. 'But even if the war ended tomorrow, after this one attack, you'd still find yourself counting those who'd died from your rifle. Your father would have a murderous son at best, a dead son at worst.'

'But you've shot, and probably killed.'

'Yes, I've shot and probably killed,' replied the young professor, 'and I already feel that I'll carry it with me for the rest of my life. If I could give you one piece of advice – just one – I'd tell you to leave. But you'd be shot immediately for desertion.'

William listened to the pump noisily sucking up water and noticed that the rain was falling less insistently. They returned to their mattresses. Most of the other soldiers were asleep. Only a few were still awake, mustering up courage for the next day. William lay down on his mattress; the mouse he now called Julius was staring at him from the corner.

'You again?' he said quietly, so as not to wake the others. 'Go away.'

He made a gesture with his hand to shoo the creature away, but Julius the mouse stayed where he was.

'Are you afraid?'

William did not know why, but the mouse no longer seemed so horrible to him. Perhaps he was very tired, or maybe the animal was hoping to be forgotten by the soldiers while the war raged on outside.

William opened his rucksack; the first thing he saw was his camera. He could have taken a photo, but then he decided that the trench was a memory he did not want to keep. He took half a rice cake from his last packet. As he held it in his hands, he thought about what the young professor had told him. He crumbled the biscuit onto the mattress and lay down, watching Julius shoving crumbs into his mouth with his little paws and swallowing them greedily, heedless of the men's presence.

*

Blackwood Jones brought in several hundred men from the second and third lines. They stood side by side facing no man's land. The sergeant began his speech, heard only by those soldiers closest to him. But his words, despite the fact that not everyone could hear, resonated with the conviction of their imminent success.

The soldiers waited well beyond dawn; the rain was still light. At one point it seemed to stop completely, and the pumps soaked up so much of the water that it only reached the top of the soldiers' boots. But then it began to fall again, even more intensely. But still not heavy enough for the sergeant to put his plan into action. It's true that he had only come up with the idea in just a few minutes the day before, without following any logical strategy. But since then, he had gone over it so many times in his mind that it now seemed infallible to him, and that everything should go as planned.

Martin hopped impatiently on the spot. He no longer bothered to wipe his glasses, convinced that his ardour was now more useful than clear, hawk-eyed vision. He was already imagining himself as a well-respected sergeant a few years from now, sitting behind a desk, with a good salary and everyone's respect. William was beside him, trying to stay focused; he had been in the trenches for less than two days, but it felt like a lifetime. He hoped that

63

the war really would be over by Christmas, as the papers had claimed for weeks now.

The young professor was nearby; instead of clutching his rifle, he held it limply. He stared down at the ground, taking deep breaths.

A little further on, William saw the former servant, Kutcher, and the student, Ericson, the two men he had shared his wine with while they wrote their postcards. They were holding on to each other, two marathon runners at the starting line, waiting for someone to give the signal.

Around midday, most of the soldiers' enthusiasm for Sergeant Blackwood Jones' plan morphed into the doubt a small cluster of them had been harbouring since dawn. They passed their time picking at lice and passing around rum, dreaming of hot barley soup. Blackwood Jones paced back and forth, beseeching the rain to co-operate.

It wasn't until evening that the wind picked up and the rain grew heavier. It was bucketing down now; thunder and lightning cracked the sky.

'For the King, the Queen and the good Lord, let's go!' Sergeant Blackwood Jones ordered.

'For the King, the Queen, and the good Lord,' replied the soldiers. William joined in with more fear than hope.

'Run as fast as you can and don't think about anything,' Martin told him, and jumped over the sandbags with an unexpectedly high leap for such a small man. William watched him disappear instantly into no man's land.

As he got up to run after him, William remembered what he had been taught the day he enrolled in the army: raise your rifle with nerves of steel, aim with nerves of steel, shoot with nerves of steel.

He wasn't sure he could do it.

He sprinted through the wall of rain, following Martin's back as if it were the North Star.

Every now and then he would turn around. Waves of soldiers soundlessly advanced, behind him, in front of him, on either side. If it hadn't been for all that rain, he might have sworn that the Germans had heard them before they saw them; but no one on the other side moved. The ground was an expanse of craters, some large, others barely wider than the men's feet. Torn tree trunks were scattered on the sodden ground – the only reminders of what must once have been a grassy plain. William kept going, sinking every couple of steps into a muddy hole or stumbling over the body of a soldier who had been dead for days. He could not tell how far he had run.

A hissing sound whistled over his head, then another.

Then the sound of machine-gun fire. He heard some of his comrades screaming, and turned around to see them fall. By the time he turned back, he could no longer see Martin ahead of him.

The young professor had also disappeared in the rain. The downpour provided little camouflage – far from it. Men were collapsing, one after the other.

Don't stop. If you stop you become a target, William said to himself again and again. He felt a stabbing pain in his leg: a bullet had flown into the flesh above his knee and burst out of the other side.

William fell into the mud, face first. Before he realised what was happening, he heard a grenade explode. The shrapnel tore through the air with the force of a hundred bullets.

Get up, soldier, William said to himself.

He put his weight on his good leg and rose to his feet, pointed his Lee–Enfield and started running again, dragging himself as best he could. He tried to take aim, but could not make out which soldiers were the enemy.

Whatever happens, shoot with nerves of steel, he told himself. Shoot.

He unloaded his rifle against the rain. His leg was burning. He had to stop for a moment to gather his strength.

A bullet grazed his arm, just below the shoulder.

He needed to breathe. To nurse the pain. His fear, which until that moment had spurred him on, had suddenly turned into a kind of miserable despair. The same despair he had felt at eight years old, when he left his mother and crossed the road to Mr Ford's bakery. He saw the carriages coming at him from both sides: the horses' hooves and carts brushed against him; a wheel bumped him and he had hit the ground. He had tried to call out for his mother, who was still talking to Dorothy Parker, but his voice had stuck fast in his throat. His lungs were constricting; he was finding it harder and harder to breathe.

'Will.' He had heard the call, but the voice was distant. He had instinctively closed his eyes.

He opened them. The road had vanished. He was still in no man's land.

There was smoke everywhere, and more soldiers on the ground than there were standing. The rest of them wandered around, disorientated, wounded.

He knew it was only a matter of time before his turn came around; a blow to the head or heart, and his life would end there, in the mud, far from home.

He thought of his father; it hurt. This pain wasn't physical, but it was more intense than his injuries. Because he was about to die without he and his father ever understanding each other. Because he would never see his father again. He would never see the girl with the North Sea in her eyes again, either. He would not save anyone, and his life would end in darkness on the battlefield.

An explosion somersaulted William Turner up into the air, then around and down into a crater full of water.

*

'Soldier.'

        'Soldier, can you hear me?'

'Turner.'

                'I'm talking to you.'

'You'd better wake up, otherwise you'll end up . . .'

'. . .'

        'Jesus Christ, it missed us by an inch.'

      'They were waiting for us. That was their plan.'

      'I'll take off my coat . . .'

'I'll make a bandage out of my shirt.'

'One second.'

'I'm almost done.'

'There. I've wrapped it around your leg.'

'Turner, all that about us running towards them. It was bullshit. They were waiting for us.'

'Turner . . .'

'TURNER!'

'Are you alive? If you are alive, give me a sign.'

'Any sign. Squeeze my hand.'

'Do something, otherwise I'll think you're dead and then I'll have to leave you here . . .'

'TURNER!'

'THEY ARE FIRING AT US.'

'. . .'

'. . .'

'This is how it is – I have to go now, boy.'

'I have to go.'

'If you can hear me, I'm so sorry, but I have to leave.'

'Edgar, is that you?'
'William.'
'They got me.'
'I know.'
'My head's spinning.'
'That's normal.'
'Am I losing a lot of blood?'
'A little.'
'Liar.'
'We have to leave and leave fast.'
'I don't think I can get up.'
'I'll help you.'
'I can't do it, Edgar.'
'You can.'
'I can't feel my leg any more.'
'You've got the other one.'
'Edgar, one thing . . .'
'What?'
'The watch – take it back to my father.'
'Forget about the watch now.'
'He'll fix it. Edgar . . .'
'Tell me.'
'You'll make an excellent sergeant.'
'Yes.'
'You won't have to carry crates any more.'
'I won't have to carry crates any more.'
'Edgar.'
'Tell me, William.'
'Will you remember me?'
'You're not dead yet.'
'I can't feel my leg any more.'

'You already said that.'

'What's it like out there?'

'Wait, I'll have a look.'

'So?'

'They're still firing.'

'I can't hear them.'

'The shots?'

'The shots.'

'They're firing everywhere, but we have to go.'

'How?'

'We're going to run.'

'Run? I can't even walk, Edgar.'

'I'll lend you my legs.'

'You know something?'

'What?'

'When you told me you had no one at home.'

'Yes.'

'They're missing out on a good friend.'

'Who knows.'

'I mean it.'

'Thank you.'

'When the war ends and you take the watch back to my father, he must know I wasn't afraid. That I died without fear and tried to save lives.'

'I won't go back, William.'

'Why?'

'Because you're coming with me now.'

'I can't do it.'

'You can do it, William. There's something you need to know, boy.'

'What, Edgar?'

'I've never had a friend, and now that I've found one, I'm not going to let him die in a puddle of mud. So you're coming with me whether you like it or not. You just have to stretch out your arm. Can you stretch your arm? That's it. Lean on your good leg. Put your weight on it. Pull yourself up. That's it. Good. Now, over my shoulder and off we go.'

Bullets flying at him from all sides, Martin ran with William clinging to his back. He was not the only one. Dozens of other soldiers, determined to save their lives, were running back towards the British trench. Many fell – almost all of them. But Martin ran with the strength of ten men. He ran fast for such a small man. The rain blurred his vision – his damned glasses – and it was no longer his enthusiasm pushing him forward, but curses, all directed towards Sergeant Blackwood Jones. He had the ardour and power of someone fighting for his life.

Martin was one of the few to reach the trench. He shakily leapt to safety but did not stop there. He kept running, crossing the first line, the second, and finally the third in the direction of the field hospital.

When they saw him arrive, exhausted, with a wounded and unconscious soldier hanging on his back, the stretcher-bearer Tyler, who recognised William because he had offered him a drink of wine, approached. Father Adams was with him; he had abandoned his beer and prayers to lend a hand.

Martin's lungs were almost empty. He used the breath he had left to alert Tyler and the chaplain to send other people to the front line. Other survivors needed help.

*

William opened his eyes. All he could see were shadows; he heard men's voices, but did not know where they were coming from. He was so weak he could not move a finger. He sensed that death wouldn't arrive like a firework, but rather a delicate absence whereby everything, little by little, faded away.

First the voices died out, then the shadows, and in the darkness, William saw a white wall.

'Why d'you keep coming back to this room, Will?' his mother asks him.

'I wanted to look at you.'

'But you can't see me very well, can you?'

'I'm forgetting you.'

'That's normal.'

'I wanted so badly to keep the promise I made you . . .'

'How much longer d'you want to live in regret? That's why you still come here. A part of you is still in the middle of that road, another part of you in this room. But I haven't been here for a long time, Will.'

'What should I do, Mum?'

'Try and understand your father before it's too late. He may not be able to change, and you have to accept it. You still have time to.'

'How?'

'You have to let me go, Will. The only way you can make me happy is to make something of your life that's valuable to you, and to those around you.'

'I've seen war. There's no valour.'

'Then don't fight any more, Will.'

Now, on the road with the exiting masses, he is walking with his new friend, Edgar Martin.

'Where are they going?' William asks.

'Away from Ypres.'

It's cold, raining, and winter is coming. Martin tells William to wait behind the bush until the procession of men and women passes. Now and then the muffled sounds of bombs can be heard.

'Edgar, what did you do before?'

'Unload crates.'

They are walking through the trees. When they stop, William takes a picture. They reach a farm and go their separate ways. William enters a house. Something happens; he does not understand. Daylight disappears, and he finds himself in darkness again. He feels the fear rising inside him when, a little further on, he sees a light.

He walks towards the light; the further he walks, the further away it seems. Of one thing he is certain: it's the light of a candle. Eventually he stops. When he does, the light comes closer and he hears a voice.

'See, William?'

'What am I supposed to see?'

'The way out.'

'I don't understand.'

'Because you're not looking properly.'

William narrows his eyes to focus. He knows there is something behind the light. The face of a girl – a beautiful girl. Her eyes are the same colour as the North Sea. He wants to dive into them. He does.

William is swimming; it's night and he's moving his arms to stay afloat. The water should be freezing, but it's not. Even though he's immersed in the North Sea, his body is dry. Only his face is wet.

'Mum,' he says.

William hears a voice: 'William.'

'Edgar, what time is it?'

'Come.'

When William opened his eyes, the first thing he saw was his friend Martin, adjusting his glasses. Then he felt a finger on his forehead and realised it was Father Adams, the chaplain, making the sign of the cross over his face before dipping his finger into a bowl of water and repeating the gesture.

William raised his arm just enough to stop him.

'I've got a feeling that I'm not dead yet, Padre,' he said, before passing out again.

*

William regained consciousness the next day. He felt exhausted, as if he could sleep for weeks. His arm was heavily bandaged. He closed his eyes, only to wake up shortly afterwards. This went on all morning.

He grew more alert in the afternoon. Two sleeping soldiers lay in neighbouring cots; he could not see beyond them. A nurse arrived to put a damp cloth on his forehead.

'Where am I?' he asked her.

'In the field hospital.'

'My head's spinning.'

'It's the fever.'

'My leg hurts.'

The nurse adjusted the gauze on his leg, returning a few minutes later to remove it.

William knew what could happen to a wound that didn't heal: gangrene. Then his leg would have to be amputated.

He turned his wrist: his watch was still in place.

'William?' It was Martin's voice. 'William, how are you?'

'You got me out of there.'

Martin held William's hand.

'I run fast. I told you I wouldn't leave you there to die.'

'Tell me one thing, but be honest.'

'Yes.'

'What's going to happen to my leg?'

'It's too early to say, even though five days have passed. Make sure you move it as much as possible.'

'Five days?'

'You were moaning constantly, they gave you morphine. You only woke up to drink water. Today is the twelfth of December.'

'Has it stopped raining?'

'Looks like it'll never stop.'

'And you . . .? Are you hurt?'

'They put a hole in my back. According to the doctor I shouldn't even be able to move. But here I am, moving.'

'A bullet?'

'Just before I came to get you. It's in there so deep they haven't even taken it out.'

'Nothing serious, is it?'

'William, the thing that will put me in the ground is still to come.'

'Edgar.'

'Yes.'

'D'you know where my rucksack is? My camera's in there, you see.'

'They brought it back here and it's safe under my bunk. You get well. In a week we'll be back on the front line, relieving the others.'

'One week?'

'Yes.'

'We'll spend Christmas on the front line?'

'That's right, William.'

'But the war should already be over by Christmas,' he said, bewildrered.

He could see them now in that very moment: the heads of governments gathered around a table, deciding to end the war, just as the newspapers had claimed for weeks.

'How are Kutcher and Ericson?'

Martin shook his head. 'They never came back.'

'Maybe they're safe somewhere.'

'The only place you can be safe is in the trench. And they aren't there, William.'

'I only spoke to them once.'

'But in some way you felt close to them, I know.'

'They were our comrades.'

Martin nodded. 'I feel the same.'

'The ones who returned . . . Us . . . They're not going to court-martial us, are they? Major Weasel mentioned that when we arrived. That's the punishment.'

'Blackwood Jones has his tail between his legs and has taken responsibility for the retreat. At the very least.'

'Just as well. And the young professor . . . How's he?'

'He's here. At the end of the third row. You can go and talk to him if you want, maybe it'll help him.'

William remembered when Major Weasel had discovered him sneaking into that very hospital at night, when he was trying to understand what the front did to the soldiers. At the time, William's questions were about the physical body. Bodies. He had wanted to know what the war had done to flesh and bone. It was only now he understood something else.

'War tears you up inside more powerfully than it does outside,' he said.

'You have to try to get back on your feet and walk again. Eat something, regain your strength. If we think about what happened, we won't be able to concentrate on the most important thing.'

'What's so important now, Edgar?'

'Survival, whatever it takes. Look what I brought you.'

Martin showed him two thick branches of wood. He had stripped off their leaves and cut them roughly to chest height. He had attached two disused rifle butts with some screws he'd got hold of in the armoury in exchange for some tobacco.

'What are they?'

'Crutches, so you can leave this stinking bunk. Every afternoon they look for volunteers to go and collect firewood. And since there's not much else to do, I go, too. The others stay behind to play cards, or to smoke, you name it. That's where I found these nice solid branches.'

Martin helped William off the bed until he was standing on one leg. He wobbled, and could have fallen over at any moment. But gradually he found his balance.

Outside the hospital, dozens of young men were bustling about in the rain. William waited for his friend to leave and concentrated on the patter of the drops, allowing all the other sounds to fade away: the groans of his wounded comrades; the muffled drumming of an anvil being beaten far away; the cries of a soldier calling for others to help him move a cart. Step by step, bed by bed, he crossed the space separating him from the door on three and a half legs.

When he was at the threshold, William took one last step and let the water run over his face. The rain was no longer his enemy on the battlefield, or his shelter. It simply gave him a sensation that might have seemed small and insignificant in most people's eyes: confirmation that he was still alive.

He returned to his bed at dinner time. He could have eaten ten portions if they had allowed it, but the nurse explained that she had been instructed to distribute only one portion per bed: a bowl of soup with some meat and a few pieces of bread.

William could not sleep that night, not just because his ailing body had done nothing else for days. It was the smell, which he was only just beginning to sense as he regained his strength. At the foot of each bed were brimming chamber pots that someone would empty sooner or later. But what about the soldiers who were unable to move and use them? How often were their sheets changed? he wondered, running his hands under his own blankets, afraid of what he might find. Luckily, they were dry. They must have washed them – though, given the scarcity of water and his itchy skin, he couldn't imagine how. As he ran his hands over his uniform, he realised that it wasn't the same one he'd been wearing the day of the attack; it was clean.

The narrow tin tub in his father's back room, which he would fill with ice-cold water for baths, now seemed like an unattainable privilege to William.

He woke up in the middle of the night and hobbled through the salty smells. When he reached the back of the third row, he called for the professor.

'Private,' the professor replied in a thin voice.

'Where are you?'

'I'm here – come forward.'

In the half-light he saw a man stretched out across the bed, with one arm and a bandage covering his entire bare chest and abdomen.

'Professor.'

'Don't say that again, soldier.'

The young professor spoke with difficulty, taking deep breaths between words.

'Why?'

'I don't think I'll be able to teach again.'

'You'll heal, Professor. If you don't give up and if you try to move a bit, you'll heal.'

Repeating the same words that Martin had said to William seemed the most reasonable thing to do.

'Stay here, keep me company.'

'I'm not leaving.'

'We should relinquish our weapons. Us, the French, the Belgians, and even the Germans. Then the war would end, because there would be no one left to fight it. We could go back to our lives – spend our Sundays in the countryside.'

'What would you do if you were over there in the countryside, Professor?'

'I'd sit on a bench.'

'And then what?'

'I'd read a book. Have you ever read a novel?'

'To tell the truth, not a whole one.'

'At least a small part of one?'

'Not even, Professor.'

'You should try to.'

William grimaced and his expression faded into the darkness. For some reason, he'd never been interested in reading, and even at school he had always struggled with textbooks. He had begun to read newspapers when the war broke out, just because everyone was talking about it, but only the articles about the front. Yet now he liked the idea of sitting on that bench with the young professor.

'When we're back home, you must recommend the best novel in the world.'

'There are so many. So many that it would take more than a lifetime to read them all.'

'I'll start with one, then.'

'It's not difficult.'

'Maybe it will be a bit. You see, I think in images more than in words.'

'What d'you like doing?'

'Photography, Professor.'

'Were you a photographer before?'

'If only. I take photographs here and there when I've got the money for film and developing.'

'What camera d'you use?'

'The one I brought with me. An old Kodak I found at a flea market. It lets you take a hundred pictures.'

'Never held a single one of those things in my hand. And tell me, why photography?'

'If someone goes away for some reason, they'll never completely disappear from your mind if you have an image of them.'

'Would you take one of me, too?'

'Tomorrow morning. A good photo needs light.'

'Did they bring you your rucksack from *The Good Pillow*?'

'Yes, thankfully.'

'What a stupid name for a dormitory, don't you think?'

'Martin says the same.'

'You two seem very close.'

'He saved my life.'

'And tell me one last thing. Did you shoot in the end?'

'Only at the rain.'

'Maybe it's for the best,' said the young professor.

*

William was woken at dawn by the thud of his rucksack on his bed.

He checked that everything was there. It was.

'I've kept a bunk for you in the dormitory,' said Martin. 'It's not too far from mine, so if you need me, just call.'

He helped William to his feet and loaded his rucksack on to his shoulders.

'One moment,' said William. 'Hand me the camera, please, and open the door to let the light in.'

William hobbled over to the young professor's bed and shook him gently. His breath was even more laboured than it had been the night before. The light illuminated his face; he was pale and sweaty.

'Professor, I'm here for the photograph.'

'Photograph . . .?' he heard him reply.

'You have to open your eyes, otherwise it won't turn out well.'

The young professor opened them wide. It seemed to William that he was making a great effort, even for such a small gesture. He framed the man's face, and when he was sure, he pressed the button.

'It'll be a good photo.'

'Of course, it will be,' said the young professor, with a hint of a smile that turned into a cough. 'As soon as you can, call the padre.'

'You're not going to die, Professor. You're very sick now, but in a few days you'll be better.'

'Call him anyway, just in case,' he said, as another cough swallowed his words.

The bunk Martin had kept for William was just three beds over from his own. William's leg still ached, but less than the day before, and his head was not spinning as intensely. He felt tired and feverish. He told Martin that he needed to sleep.

He only rose for his rations and to line up at the latrine. Before returning to the dormitory, William approached Father Adams and warned him that the young professor wanted to see him. In the dorm, he heard the soldiers moving around, these sounds only ceasing after nightfall.

The war seemed so far away from his bed. He remembered that he was still hungry, and that he had some biscuits. When he took out the packet, he discovered they were almost all gone. At that same moment, two little eyes popped out of his rucksack, curious to see who had taken their food without asking.

'Julius,' said William. 'Have you been in there all this time, little man?'

The mouse jumped on to the bed. It hovered between the covers and stopped to rest next to the packet with the remaining crackers. Soon afterwards, William closed his eyes for the umpteenth time.

When he opened them again, he felt stronger. His fever was almost gone and the wound on his leg no longer throbbed. He still needed crutches to move, but was able to place his foot on the ground a bit more and even take a few small steps.

In the daylight, despite the grey mist on the horizon and the cold, William could almost smell spring, light and fresh.

He watched his comrades. Except for a few chores, which might take up to two or three hours a day, away from the front line they went back to being young men who played cards and joked. A few of the more daring soldiers improvised a game of football in the rain; the ball was made of rolled-up rags. William spied a group of new recruits, receiving orders from Foster. They were full of the faith in the war that he'd once had.

It took William a few more days to fully recover. Then his legs carried him everywhere, and his crutches lay at the foot of his bunk like old and useless tools. He spent his days like the others, counting the hours and hoping that the sun would grace them with its presence before they returned to the mud of the trenches. Even if it was only for an hour.

Early in the morning and after lunch, he visited the young professor's bedside. He was in a stable condition, but no one knew if he would recover. Sometimes he recognised William; other times he moaned in pain, unaware that someone was at his bedside.

He had only spoken to the chaplain twice. Father Adams went to great lengths with the nurses to keep the wounded in the field hospital in a decent condition, changing blood-soaked bandages, and washing clothes and sheets for those who could not use the chamber pots. The first time William thanked him for taking care of him when he was unconscious, Adams only responded with a nod. The second time, as he carried a pile of sheets from the hospital that looked as though they had come out of the latrine hole, the chaplain replied, 'God is gambling with too many young men's lives, and I'm losing my patience with Him.' He was disappointed rather than angry.

William spent a lot of time with Julius the mouse; the other soldiers had come to see it as William's bizarre pet. The mouse even slept on his bed, no longer fearing that someone would kick it off. During mealtimes it sometimes rested on William's shoulder, waiting for a piece of the soupy bread ration.

Martin was one of the few young men, in those days, waiting impatiently to return to the front line and prove his worth. His future depended on it, he would tell William over and over. As if his success in battle would lead to a real job, in the army, once the war was over.

Unlike many others, who had someone waiting for them at home, Martin had found his purpose in the army. The army had given him direction, and he was acutely aware – more than most people – that real hunger was far worse than the slop they were served here every day. He was not, however, a sociable member of the group. He had never played cards in his life, nor was he good with a ball, and to keep moving, he went out in the afternoons to fetch wood.

As William continued to rest and regain his strength, Martin's kindling expeditions tapered off. Gathering wood so regularly had exacerbated the twinges in his back; it sometimes left him paralysed and in deep pain, despite his strong build.

One evening, around a fire that sputtered in the rain, Martin told William, 'There are only three days left until we finally leave.'

'I need to be honest with you. I hope that day doesn't ever come.'

'What are you thinking?'

'What we are doing here . . .? Killing or being killed . . . What's the point, Edgar? I don't know what came over me when I left. We should lay down our weapons, like the young professor said. If everyone did that, then the war really would be over by Christmas.'

'You must have hit your head very hard when that grenade exploded next to you. D'you remember what happens to those who disobey orders? You risk being shot. Let's not talk about it any more. Come on.' Martin walked away, stating that he really needed to stretch his legs.

William spent most of the next day alone, sitting under a sheltering canopy.

Father Adams was the first to approach him.

'I've always liked to think of them as God's tears,' he said, pointing to the rain. 'Tears of joy in summer, that refresh the air and revive the plants in the fields. Tears of sorrow for our behaviour when the rain is very heavy, causing damage to houses and inundating rivers. But now that I'm looking at it, I see something else entirely.'

'What do you see?'

'Rain. There is no God in this water that's been pouring down on us for days. I don't understand his business, but by now I think he's forgotten about this part of the world.'

'Why d'you say that, Padre?'

'Because with each passing day, I see more and more clearly that the deaths of all these boys are meaningless. I agreed to come here to bring comfort to the soldiers. I trusted that God would end the war immediately. Even if it's true that no war is just, we did begin this one to defend an innocent population – the intent was just. I was with the young professor just now when he took his last breath.'

'He's dead . . .?'

William wanted to say more, but the words stuck hard in his throat.

'He told me to give you this,' said Father Adams.

He pulled out a pipe from his tunic, along with a packet of tobacco, and handed it to William. William weighed it in his hands before slipping it into his coat pocket.

'He wanted you to smoke it on a bench. He used those very words – "on a bench". D'you know what he was referring to?'

'I do.'

The young professor was dead, and with him he had taken all the novels he had read and all the novels he would have recommended to William. All the novels he was yet to read; all the lectures he would have given to his students when he returned from the war; all the Sundays spent in the middle of a meadow, sitting on a bench: gone. All that remained of him was that pipe and a photograph imprinted on the film in William's camera: black and white, still to be developed.

The soldiers gathered at sunset. Father Adams said a prayer for those who had not made it. He concluded with a blessing. At dinner-time, William gave some food to Edgar Martin. Since arriving in Ypres, he had lost a lot of weight. But he hardly cared about eating any more. All he could think about was that which now seemed so obvious to him: the war would not save anyone. William wondered why he hadn't realised this earlier, and why the young professor, who was much wiser than him, hadn't realised it either. He could have been at home at that moment, after a day's lectures, reading one of his novels in a comfortable armchair. And William could have been rushing through the streets of the city, delivering packages of repaired watches that people would give to their loved ones. He could have eaten late in the evening with his father – the wordless clinking of plates and forks – and he might have welcomed that silence, rather than resenting it. Accepted it, as one accepts the rising tide when the wind blows. They might understand each other. It is in understanding that fears vanish, that the doors of the moment we are living in open wide. And those of the past close shut. If a simple bucket cannot empty a trench of mud, it's much better to get out of the trench.

Martin tapped him on the shoulder.

'You need to move,' he said. 'Come and fetch wood with me.'

'I'd prefer to stay here.'

'It's not far, boy. An hour there and another one back. That way you can test your leg, see if it works. You wouldn't want it to give up on you while you're running into battle, would you? Better to know beforehand.'

'Where did you say the place is?'

'I never told you, actually. It's a forest.'

'A forest?'

'Ploegsteert Forest.'

THREE

Flanders, 1933

'WAS HIS LEG ALL RIGHT?' the boy asked. 'Was he able to walk to the forest?'

'What you really want to know is whether William Turner managed to find the girl with the North Sea in her eyes isn't it?'

'Um . . . yes, I do.'

It had been months since they had spent a whole day together, just the two of them, and this was the first time in as long as the man could remember that they were really talking. He noticed that the boy's gaze was beginning to grow into that of the adult he would become in a few years. He was about to answer the question when he saw two figures dressed in long coats approaching.

'Come here,' he told the boy. 'Whatever they say, I'll do the talking.'

'What do they want?'

'I don't know yet.'

They waited for them to arrive. One of the figures was tall and thin, the other stocky and rosy-cheeked, from the wind or wine.

The taller one addressed them in French, but the boy's father was unable to understand and so he answered in his own language.

'Germans, are you?' the stocky one asked.

The man nodded.

'I speak your language. What are you doing in these parts, may I ask?'

'We're on a special trip. I'm taking my son here to see the battlefields.'

'Did you fight in the Great War?'

'I did.'

The stocky man translated for the tall one, who nodded and scrutinised father and son with a stern look.

'So, we were enemies,' said the stocky man.

'We were,' nodded the boy's father. 'And I hope we won't be again.'

The stocky man took a flask out of his coat pocket, unscrewed the cork and took a drink, wiping his lips with his sleeve. The tall man asked him to pass it over, but before he drank, whispered something into the other's ear.

'We would like to see your documents.'

'Have we done something wrong?' asked the man.

'It's just a check. We've been notified by your government. It seems quite a few Germans are leaving Germany. Some of them end up here, in Flanders.'

The man shuddered and squeezed the boy's shoulder with his good hand. The tall man noticed.

'It's just me and my son.'

He handed over his documents to the tall man, who carefully checked them before passing them to his fellow official.

'They seem fine. I told my colleague that you didn't look like the people they'd described to us.'

'I don't quite understand,' said the man. 'What kind of people are you looking for?'

'Jews.'

'We're not Jewish.'

'Let's be clear,' the stocky man began to explain. 'Neither of us have anything against Jews. We're just doing checks.'

'I see.'

'You know that a long time ago many men fought here, in this place,' the stocky man said to the boy.

'We wanted to get to the North Sea and you blocked us.'

'The North Sea . . . That's right. I see you know the story, you're a good boy. I fought, too, but several miles from here. You never did manage to get there,' said the stocky man with a hint of pride.

'Who knows, sooner or later we may succeed,' the boy's father responded.

The stocky officer took another swig from his flask and put it back in his coat pocket. The tall man yawned and made a gesture for them to leave.

'My colleague can't stand it when I stand around chatting. Everything is in order here, anyway.'

He returned their documents and they all said goodbye. The man and his son silently stared at the two men until they disappeared into the distance.

'Dad, what have the Jews done?'

'They haven't done anything, son.'

'So why are they looking for them?'

'I can't answer that, I'm sorry.'

'It's because of that man in the government, isn't it?'

'If nobody listened to him, he would just be a man ranting into the wind. He'll never change – he's been like this ever since he was a soldier.'

'You know him?'

'I fought with him.'

'Here?' the boy asked, astonished.

'Yes, right here. He was a young corporal, a messenger.'

The boy bowed his head.

'Those two reminded me of the young men who stopped us near our house a few weeks ago. But this was just a standard check, right?'

The man nodded, ruffling the boy's hair in an attempt to reassure him there was nothing to fear. But the two men who had just left had also reminded him of the same frightening episode.

The man had been on his way home from the bakery with his son when it happened. It was Sunday, and he had bought some cake as well as the bread for the holy day. A few boys had approached them on the road home. They must have been nineteen, twenty years old, the same age the man had been when he left for the war. One of them had said to the others, 'That's him.'

'You think we don't know what you think?' he had said, squaring up to the man and shoving him. The package slipped from the man's hands, a slice of cake breaking free and tumbling to the ground. 'Look at him, the man who preaches against war,' the boy had said to his cronies. 'This is just a warning. There's no place here for the likes of you. What you did at Ypres is a disgrace to all Germans. If we see you or any of your family around, you won't be so lucky next time.'

They had sloped off. The man had picked up his parcel. The two remaining slices for his son and wife were intact. He had let go of his own slice.

'I'm scared, Dad. What did they want from you?'

'They think they can get everything they want by bullying. They're boys who dream of going to war one day, without the slightest idea of what it means. And they hate anyone who thinks differently. Unfortunately, there are more and more of them.'

'You never told me about the war.'

'Come on, let's go, Mum's waiting for us.'

'See, they're not coming back. It really was just a standard check as the man said.'

The boy felt calm again. He pointed to the sky. 'Look, the clouds are filling the sky.'

'Maybe we still have time to finish our story.'

'We were at the part where Martin asks William to go with him into Ploegsteert Forest,' the boy prompted.

'Where I met William Turner for the first time.'

Flanders, 1914

APART FROM WILLIAM TURNER and Edgar Martin, the six soldiers marching to the forest knew one another only by sight. They had survived the attack in no man's land and were still recovering from their wounds. As they marched, they wondered what their first Christmas at war would be like.

One of them had heard from the communications officers that gift parcels were on their way from Princess Mary. And some soldiers were even expecting parcels from their families.

William wanted ham for Christmas, but he knew that his father would not send him anything; money was scarce. Even before his departure, there had been far fewer customers bringing watches to the shop.

'What are you thinking about?' asked Martin.

'Ham.'

'What kind of a thought is that?' he asked, laughing.

'When I left, my father gave me a piece of ham, but someone stole it from me on my way here.'

'You'll eat it when we go home. How's your leg?'

'It's still pretty sore, but I can walk on it.'

Only a few drops of rain filtered through the tall foliage. The paths all looked the same, covered in shadows as the day drew to an end.

Martin took the trouble to explain to William how to secure a bundle of kindling, by weaving two pieces of twine together at the ends of the branches. This made it easier to carry. The men would split up into three pairs, as per their instructions.

The first pair manned the cart and the other two set out to gather wood. Finding it was not difficult – there were so many branches on the ground. They would make a good fire once they were dry. They picked up the wood, weaved them into bundles and continued.

After an hour the cart was half full. Martin suggested they split up and pointed two of the pairs towards a path, explaining that he and William would take the one next to it.

Once they were walking, William noticed that Martin was having trouble bending over.

'What is it, Edgar?'

'My back's really starting to hurt.'

'I'll fetch the branches, you just stay here and prepare the bundles.'

It wasn't a good idea to be alone, especially in a forest, but the pain in Martin's back was so bad it prevented him from thinking straight.

'Go, William, but make sure you don't stray too far.'

William was certain that one of these days, perhaps even this very night, he would escape the war. Along with the girl he had met in the abandoned house, if he ever found her again. And he would reach the North Sea. From there, he could board a ship and return to his father's workshop in England. He would talk to him. That was the only gift he really wanted – much more than a piece of ham – but he still struggled to admit it to himself. He wanted to get home before 3 January, his father's birthday. He would ask to learn his father's trade, and with a little practice, his mother's watch would work again. Perhaps, along with the watch, everything else would be fixed, and the war would gradually become a distant memory.

William walked on, forgetting about the kindling, moonlight beaming through the gaps in the clouds, marking out the silhouettes of the trees. He couldn't see much further than about ten paces ahead. The only sounds, muffled and distant, were those of explosions.

When they, too, ceased, silence fell. He was tired. He didn't know if it was his leg, or the pressure of sadness lodged at the base of his sternum that was making it hard to breathe. He paused by a tree, shrugged off his rucksack and sat down to rest.

Julius the mouse peeked out of his bag, poking his nose into the air, as though he might catch a scent of something that was imperceptible to humans. He looked at William. They looked at each other: a man and a mouse on the edges of the war.

'There are no more crackers,' William said. 'There's no more of anything for us, my friend.'

Julius leapt out of the rucksack, hopped around, jumped up onto William's legs and into his open palm. William brought him closer and stroked his small head with one tender finger.

'How did you end up in the trenches? Did you run away from something, or were you there before it all started, Julius?'

The mouse barely moved.

'Yes, we may never know.'

When he felt rested, William tucked Julius back into his rucksack. He abandoned the path and walked through the undergrowth; a fugitive could hide in this thick undergrowth. He didn't know where he was going, but he knew that he had to keep on.

He walked for a long time, finding nothing but trees and bushes, when he noticed something on the ground. It was a blanket. He picked it up. The ground beneath was a little hollowed out, as if someone had been sleeping there for a while.

'Hey,' he called in a low voice.

Silence.

'Is it you? If it's you, show yourself.'

Silence.

'It's William Turner.'

He heard a footstep.

He was afraid, but the desire to find the girl was stronger than his fear and urged him on, one step after another, his rifle pointed. Until, behind a tree, he saw some light. He approached, trying not to make any noise.

When he reached the tree, he became convinced the light was coming from a candle. With a jerk, he leapt around the tree and pointed his rifle.

The girl with the North Sea in her eyes was sitting on the ground, trembling. She lifted her gaze and seemed to look straight into the barrel of the rifle, then she shifted her gaze to William.

'William,' she said, smiling.

Barely a stub was left of the candle she had taken from the abandoned house. A blanket, similar to the one on the ground, hung around her shoulders. William wondered where she had found it – if someone had given it to her on the way, or if she had taken them from another abandoned house. She was even thinner than when he had first met her.

'Here, I'll try and light it,' he said, reaching for the tiny candle.

He patted the ground, finding a flattish plain upon which to place the candle.

'Ploegsteert,' said the girl, pointing to the woods.

'Yes, Ploegsteert,' William said. He remembered that he had a woollen jumper in his rucksack, which he retrieved.

The girl grabbed it and put it on, thanking him with her eyes. Sea foam swam in her pupils.

'You're shaking.'

William sat down beside the girl, put his arm around her. She huddled closer, as if for protection. From the cold and the war.

'Are you hungry?' he asked her.

She did not reply.

In his rucksack, he still had the tins of meat he had received at headquarters before leaving for the front. Now, he opened one for her.

The girl with the North Sea in her eyes slipped two fingers inside and brought the food to her mouth with the greed of someone who has not eaten for days. When she had finished, she sucked her fingers. Her face and arms were dirty, but he still found her beautiful. She had the beauty of forgotten things.

At that moment, Julius the mouse jumped out of the rucksack and scurried onto William's shoulder. He must have smelled the food.

'He's a friend of mine,' William told the girl, pointing to the mouse. 'His name's Julius, you don't need to be afraid.'

But she didn't seem afraid. She let Julius lick the tin can, and he let her pet him gently. Then he scampered back into William's rucksack.

Then the candle began to flicker and the wind blew it out. They stayed there, embracing, until she fell asleep in his arms.

I will take you away from here, he thought. We'll abandon the war this very night and make it to the North Sea. I'll introduce you to my father, I'm sure he'll be pleased. But we must hurry, so that we can be far away before dawn.

He closed his eyes for a few minutes, too, to regain his strength. Then he shook himself and got up. He nudged the girl gently to wake her.

'We have to leave,' he said.

Silence.

He mimed footsteps in the air with his fingers, in the direction of the North Sea.

The girl looked at him, trying to understand what he was saying. She pulled out the map he had given her at the abandoned house and placed it in the palm of his hand so that he could feel, in the darkness, the texture of the paper. She, too, mimed footsteps with her fingers and said something in her own language. William realised it was another word for the sea.

*

William had to do this. For himself, for his father. And for that girl who clung to his arm because she had nothing left but a dream of the sea.

She was so fragile. So thin and full of fear. That's what war does to people, he thought; it diminishes them.

Yet they clung to hope, a waning candle that continued to flicker inside them. They had to keep going to make sure it did not go out.

They walked slowly; his leg was beginning to give up on him and she hardly had any strength left.

Every now and then she murmured his name: 'William.' That was all.

William pulled her closer whenever she said his name. He was beginning to convince himself that deserting was the right choice. He could make out her gaze in the darkness – it made a noise, like the waves – but he could no longer see the colour of her eyes.

After all, even the sea is invisible in the dark.

A short time had passed when he heard a crunching sound, as if someone was snapping branches nearby. He paused to listen, motioning to the girl to be quiet. For a few minutes, Ploegsteert Forest plunged into silence. When snapping sounds came again, William pulled the girl behind a tree and crouched down beside her.

'William,' she whispered.

He brought his index finger to his mouth.

'Don't speak.'

He thought he heard voices approaching. His heart raced. The girl clutched him even tighter.

Two German soldiers.

In the half-light, he realised their silhouettes were no more than twenty paces away. They had stopped to discuss something in a grassy clearing, surrounded by sparse trees; through the gaps, moonbeams lit them up. One was holding an empty tin of meat in his hand. He was a scrawny, malnourished man with thin hair combed to one side and dark, hungry eyes. He was straining them, even in the half-light. His facial features were tightly drawn into a smirk of satisfaction.

He was talking excitedly to his companion, as though a sudden fever had driven him to delirium. He gesticulated, twirling the small tin box in the air and pointing several times in the opposite direction to where William and the girl were crouched.

The other man pointed his finger at the tree, muttering something that William could not hear.

All he understood was that they could not agree on which direction to take. Still hidden from view, William raised his rifle and aimed it. The soldier who had pointed towards them was obscured by a bush, but he had a clear view of the other one.

He was aiming straight for the man's head. But something held him back. If he fired, the soldier's comrade would realise where they were hiding and attack them. Or he'd run off and shout for reinforcements. If he did not shoot, perhaps the first soldier would win the discussion and they would leave, and he and the girl would be able to continue their journey to the North Sea.

He chose to wait. The men continued to argue animatedly, then the soldier with the small box in his hand suddenly marched away and William lost his firing position. The other stayed where he was. As if he could sense them, he pointed his rifle and approached.

'You have to go,' he told the girl. 'I'll take care of him.'
'William.'

'You have to run as fast as you can.'

He pointed her in the right direction. She shook her head, telling him she didn't want to leave.

'Go!'

He put the remaining tins from his rucksack into her lap. He peeked around the tree and saw that the German soldier was only a few yards away.

He looked into her eyes and she finally understood that her presence would put him in even more danger. She kissed him, a salty kiss, mixed with tears. A kiss that could have gone on forever. It tasted like the sea.

The girl started to run with the last of her strength. The German soldier moved at full speed and was immediately on top of her. He raised his rifle, shouting something in German. The girl turned around. The rifle was pointed at her forehead. She froze in fear.

He'll kill her, thought William, because he's a German soldier, and that's what Germans do – they kill people.

He could easily take aim from his position, shoot him in the back, no problem. He pointed his rifle, placed his finger on the trigger and applied light pressure. Only then did he ask himself if other German soldiers were also out on patrol. William couldn't hear any noises. Just wind and rain. Yet the sound of a gun, in the silence of the forest, would travel far, and another German comrade would hear it. They would be faster than a girl who could hardly stay on her feet and a soldier with a wounded leg. They would catch them.

William realised the only thing he could do was to try and protect the girl. She was like a plant at the mercy of the rain, that girl. He realised then that saving someone else is even more difficult than saving oneself at times.

He moved towards the German soldier, who was still aiming his rifle at the girl. It was as if he didn't know what to do now, because none of his superiors had imagined such a scenario. He felt as if he was watching a scene in which he had played a part only two weeks earlier: going up to the attic in the abandoned house and pointing his own rifle at the girl.

The German soldier seemed to sense his presence. The moment before the barrel of William's rifle touched his back, he abruptly turned around.

An Englishman and a German, pointing their rifles at each other.

In the German's grim face, obscured in the half-light, William saw his own fear reflected. 'Shoot them before they shoot you,' Martin had told him as they had tramped through the countryside; it seemed like a thousand years ago now. 'If you shoot someone, you'll take them with you forever,' the young professor had told him.

If one of them fired, the other might, in the short time left to him, instinctively fire back. Both William and the German soldier realised this.

The German spoke first.

All he said was, 'Calm down.' He said it in English.

'Lower your rifle,' William replied.

'I can't.'

'All I want to do is leave with her.' William pointed at the pleading girl.

'Where d'you want to go?'

'Away from here.'

104

'You can't,' said the German soldier. 'Our camp is nearby. And there are others on patrol. You wouldn't make it out alive.'

'Put the rifle down.'

'I can't.'

'How come you can speak English?'

'I used to work in London, before the war.'

'What did you do in London?'

'I was a waiter in a restaurant.'

William tried to imagine the man weaving through tables in his white waiter's uniform. He struggled to reconcile this vision with that of the soldier in front of him.

'What's your name?'

'Carl Mühlegg. And yours?'

'William Turner,' he said, and had a strange sensation.

Obviously the soldier had a name, but hearing him pronounce it suddenly made him more of a person.

'Where did your comrade go?'

'He's convinced that some of your companions are hiding in the forest. Are they?'

William did not reply. He did not want him to know that he and the girl were alone in the Ploegsteert woods.

'At least let her leave.' He nodded towards the girl. 'She has nothing to do with any of this.'

Carl Mühlegg lowered his forehead.

'She could go and tell someone.'

'She can't even stand up. Look at her.'

The German soldier turned, for a moment, towards the girl. She was dragging herself, with enormous effort, into a bush; a desperate attempt to take cover.

'How d'you know her?'

105

'She was hiding in an abandoned house. She's part of the group of evacuees from Ypres.'

'Where did you want to go with her, soldier?'

'To the North Sea.'

'You're a deserter,' said Carl Mühlegg. The situation suddenly became clear to him.

'I'm just tired of the war.'

'We all are.'

'I don't believe you, Mühlegg. We're fighting to defend Europe from the likes of you.'

'We believe the same thing, you know. I just want peace to come soon.'

Peace. That was the reason William had gone to war. To bring about peace. At the very least to find some peace inside himself.

'There is no peace in war,' William said instinctively.

'Why don't you stop, then?'

'Because you've entered land that doesn't belong to you. You should go home.'

'This land doesn't belong to the British either,' said Carl Mühlegg, gripping his rifle even tighter.

William did the same in response. He knew they couldn't go on like this. Sooner or later one of them would shoot, to save himself, and the other would shoot back instinctively. Yet as he spoke to the soldier, he realised that he was a boy, just like him, trying not to die.

At the same time, however, he knew he would have to kill Carl Mühlegg, just as Carl knew he would have to kill William. William wondered how he could shoot a man who was standing in front of him, with whom he had just spoken the truth.

The soldiers stayed there, in the chill of the night, waiting. Neither of them knew what they were waiting for. William hoped that Martin was searching for him, that he would suddenly leap out of the bushes. Mühlegg was hoping the same thing about his own comrade; but neither of them appeared.

*

The soldiers stayed standing, stock-still, pointing their rifles. They began to feel exhausted and cold, and William's leg was aching.

It was Carl Mühlegg who broke the silence.

'How far have you walked?'

'No idea. Far, I'd say.'

'This forest is only a hundred hectares.'

'So?'

'It means you've been going round in circles.'

'Your comrade should be back by now. If the forest is as small as you say, my comrades will surely have caught him, and they'll be coming back for me.'

'Or he went back to the camp alone. It wouldn't be the first time.'

'I saw you arguing just now.'

'He's been at the front for a while. Since the October battle . . . You know about it, right?'

'I read about it in the papers.'

'He was a messenger, running from the rear to the front line, heedless of everyone. He spends the whole day alone, on the sidelines, and can't bear to go on night inspections with his comrades.'

'If we stay like this, we'll freeze to death.' William sat down on the grass, still pointing his rifle. His leg was too sore to stand on now.

'What time is it?' asked Carl Mühlegg.

William looked at his watch. 'It's broken.'

'Why d'you wear such a small watch? It looks like it was made for a woman's wrist.'

'It was my mother's.'

Carl Mühlegg thought of his own mother. She was at home, in Germany, waiting for him to return. She had sent him a postcard – *Carl, I'm waiting for you* – as if it was up to him as to when he returned. He missed his home and family, and felt close to the British soldier.

'Is that why you were running away? To get back to your mother?'

'She's dead. This watch is all I have left of her.'

'How did that happen?'

William told him about the accident. It felt very strange to be recounting this episode to a German. Yet there was something inside him that drove him on. He was tired of being a soldier, of the war.

'All that for a piece of cake,' Carl Mühlegg finally said.

'Exactly.'

'I'm sorry, Turner.'

'Coming from someone who has a gun pointed at me, I find that hard to believe.'

'This rifle is just circumstance.'

'That could send us both to the next life.'

'We don't choose our circumstances – you must grant me that. Even the story you told me . . . A bad circumstance. You know, I don't think life is what happens to us. Maybe it's nothing more than our reaction to those circumstances.'

'You might be right, Mühlegg.'

William closed his eyes. Was that the North Sea he could smell in the wind? It reminded him of the time he had visited the sea with his parents as a child. The same smell was in the air when he had crossed the Channel to join the war effort. His leg would not be able to take him there; it was becoming clearer and clearer to him as the pain intensified. But maybe the girl would make it. She had managed to reach the forest and, with a bit of luck, she might carry on without being caught. All the way to the sea. He lowered his rifle and threw it to one side.

'There, now you can do what you want,' he told Carl Mühlegg. 'You can return to your base with a prisoner and be covered in honours. At least let her go.'

Carl Mühlegg came closer to William. 'On your feet, soldier,' he said. William struggled to rise; the German soldier's rifle was pressing into his chest. 'Now turn around and continue in that direction,' he continued, pointing to the bush where the girl had gone to hide.

When they arrived, they realised she had disappeared. William stuck his hands into the brambles and pushed his way in, followed by Carl Mühlegg, who continued to hold him at gunpoint. He noticed the flap of her blanket hanging from a branch.

'I think she's run away,' he said, and something clenched in his heart.

'Let's go back,' Carl Mühlegg ordered.

As he limped on, William wondered if she was still there; if she was still watching them from another, better vantage point, or was already far away. He hoped that she would arrive at her destination. Perhaps she would think of him when she opened the tins of meat. And wait for him, on a beach by the North Sea. But he was in too much pain; even returning to camp would be a great feat. And now that he was at gunpoint, he was no longer able to make any decisions at all.

He had followed the young professor's advice. The moment we lay down our arms, war ceases to exist. At least for him, at that moment. He would have liked his father to have seen him, to be proud of his son just for once.

Carl Mühlegg urged him towards the clearing where he had paused, an hour earlier, to argue with his comrade.

He ordered William to stop.

'You can only fight a war if there's an enemy, and I don't see one in front of me.'

William turned around to find that Carl Mühlegg had lowered his rifle.

'I don't see one either. That's why I laid down my own gun.'

'Go and fetch it, then go back to your camp. This is the shortest route. I hope you'll find a way to see your father again, and I hope I'll see my family, too.'

William nodded.

'But if I find you in my path again, I won't hesitate to shoot you.'

'Me neither,' said William and hobbled away, without saying another word.

*

The camp was a two-hour walk from the clearing. William dragged his battered leg behind him, using his rifle as a stick. Whenever he heard a sound, he took cover behind a tree, afraid that he might encounter other German soldiers. But he didn't come across anyone at all. They were just frightened animals scurrying away from the sound of his footsteps.

William would never be able to return to the woods to look for the girl. In two days, he would be sent back to the front line: to kill or be killed. The desolation of the trenches stretched far beyond the channels dug into the earth. It had entered him – entered all of them. There was no escaping it.

When the two hours were up, William was still only halfway there, just outside the forest. He urged himself to keep strong and keep moving. He knew that his leg could give way at any moment, and he almost hoped it would. His vision was blurred; the cold was burrowing into his bones. Not far from the camp, he accidentally plunged his foot into a hole.

He lay spreadeagled on the ground. Sharp needles of freezing cold rain soaked his face, his coat, his rifle. His vision blurred, until he could only see one colour – the white of the walls.

The bed where his mother lay motionless appeared in front of him.

'Will, you're back.'

'I'm tired and I need to rest. Make some room for me, so I can lie down next to you.'

'If you do that, you won't be able to get up this time. You know that, right?'

'I know.'

'And is this what you want? To abandon your life for this room?'

'I have no strength left.'

'You can find new strength. Every one of us has hidden resources that help us handle the most difficult situations.'

'I tried tonight. I tried so hard. The North Sea . . . it's still so far away.'

'Then maybe that's not where you need to go, Will.'

He takes a few steps towards the bed. The soft sheets are so inviting, tempting him to lie down next to his mother and fall asleep forever. He sinks his hand into the mattress. It's so soft.

Before lying down, William turns towards the door. He thinks he can hear a soft but sharp sound beyond it, calling to him. He moves closer, puts his ear to the door. The sound is clearer now. He pushes down the handle and opens it.

Julius the mouse is on the ground in front of him, standing on two paws.

'You came all the way here?'

The mouse leaps up, jumps on to his leg and crawls up to his shoulder.

He points to the corridor with his snout, William sees a light at the end.

'I don't know if I can do this, Julius.'

His mother is still watching him. He would like to say something to her, but he does not. She's the one to talk.

'You made me a promise, remember? You left to save people. There's still time, Will. All you must do is leave this room.'

The contours of her face blur.

William hesitates on the threshold.

Then he crosses it.

'You'll always be in my heart, Mum,' he says, 'even when the memories are gone. I promise.'

He leaves and pulls the door behind him. He walks all the way down the corridor.

William looked up into the trees from his position on the ground. Julius was crawling along his forehead, squeaking. William took him into his hands and sat up.

'We're not far from the camp now,' he said.

He stood up. Before setting off, he tried to put Julius back in his rucksack, but for the first time ever the mouse refused. He crawled down William's arm, and jumped to the ground. Julius scampered away, turned around and then moved off again.

'You want to leave, don't you? I can't go with you. My leg really hurts. I'd follow you if I could. But I can't. Listen, you'll do well in the forest, even without me. You'll be free. Go.'

And off the mouse went, scurrying towards the path. He stopped once more.

'Run as far as you can, my friend.'

Julius squealed and disappeared into the grass.

William stood there for a while, tracing an imaginary line from the point where Julius had disappeared all the way to the sea. The North Sea.

Then he pointed his rifle at the ground and, using it as a crutch, returned to his comrades.

*

Major Weasel came to wake him up late that morning, accompanied by two privates.

'With me, Turner,' he said.

The soldiers standing either side of Weasel held their rifles tightly, the barrels aimed up. William picked up his clothes from the floor and hastily shoved them on. He limped out of the dormitory, his comrades watching him. He passed by Martin's bunk, noticing that it was empty.

They walked through the camp in the rain, past the hospital, then the latrine area, on to a narrow path leading to the major's quarters.

Weasel wiped his boots on a rag at the entrance. William and the two soldiers did the same, so as not to displease the major before the interrogation had even begun.

Weasel pointed to a wooden chair.

'Make yourself comfortable,' he said sarcastically.

William sat down. A warm fire was crackling in the open fireplace.

Weasel opened a large register on which he noted the day's date and time.

'The nineteenth of December, 1914, 11.45. Interrogation number 92. Private William Turner. Witnesses, Privates Fisher and Grant.'

He raised his head from the register. His black eyes looked everywhere and nowhere all at once, just like those of a weasel.

'Well, Turner, we can begin. Please answer my questions precisely. Last night, six soldiers, including you, went to collect wood in the nearby Ploegsteert Forest, under my authorisation. Do you confirm?'

'Confirmed, sir.'

114

'Five of them returned, more than an hour late. The versions of all five match up. They looked for you, couldn't find you and returned to camp, assuming you would be there. Only you were not at the camp.'

'No, sir.'

'And where, pray tell, were you, Turner?'

'Still in the woods.'

'Can you explain what you were doing alone in the woods, when you had been given orders to stay close to at least one other soldier.'

'I got lost, sir. We split into pairs. My comrade was suffering from severe back pain and was no longer able to proceed. I offered to go on alone, but I got lost.'

'You are telling me you got lost in a two-hundred-and-fifty-acre forest, Turner?'

'Exactly.'

'One might say you have a German's sense of direction.'

'Excuse me?'

'Germans are well known for having no sense of direction. Are you a German, Private Turner?'

'No, sir. Never, sir.'

'And what did you do when you got lost?'

'At first, I despaired and waited for my comrades, hoping they would come looking for me. Then, as time passed, I assumed they had returned to the camp, so I tried to find my own way back.'

'You found it, I see.'

'Only after many hours. My injured leg slowed me down really badly, sir.'

'Private Turner?'

Weasel's eyes flashed like the embers in the fireplace.

'Yes, sir.'

'This is not the first war I have been involved in, and it certainly won't be the last. Over the years, I have learned that every good officer should remain calm. It's a demanding exercise, you know? If there's one thing that I'm not particularly fond of, it's being irritated, which leads to a loss of self-control, and this loss of self-control leads to making instinctive decisions. Would you like me to make an instinctive decision about your fate at this time, Private Turner?'

'No, sir.'

'Since we agree, I'll ask the question one last time. What did you do in the woods for all those hours?'

'I was lost, Major.'

Weasel leaned forward. His eyes came so close to William's face that he felt engulfed by their darkness. The major slammed his hand down on the table, hard.

'I want to know about the Germans!'

'What do you want to know, Major?'

'If you came into contact with the Germans and released vital information about the organisation of our camp.'

William Turner shivered. He tried to remain calm.

'I didn't meet any Germans, sir. If that had happened, I wouldn't be here talking to you. They are as mean and merciless as ferocious animals, everyone knows that. But I would certainly have taken at least four or five of them with me before I died.'

'That they are like ferocious animals, without humanity or reason, there is no doubt,' Weasel said. 'Before this interrogation ends, and I make my decision about your fate, is there anything else you would like to add?'

116

William tried to read the major's thoughts, but his gaze was impenetrable. What did Weasel want to hear? If he told him he had run into a German soldier while he'd been trying to desert, Weasel would have him shot for treason. He knew that the major did not entirely believe him – he could feel it – but no one had seen him with Carl Mühlegg. He had to say something that would at least make him seem sincere.

'Yesterday, at the field hospital, a soldier I had befriended while fighting on the front line died. That was all I could think about when I wandered into the woods, and I lost my way.'

'You put the lives of your comrades at risk. Are you aware of that?'

'I know, sir. I won't be forgiven for that.'

Weasel's eyes flashed, staring at William and the rest of the room at the same time.

'I'll try and believe you, Turner,' he said, 'but I can't easily overlook what you did. To make up for your error, you'll be on lookout on Christmas night. So, it is decided.' He set about writing some notes on a sheet of paper, which he secured with sealing wax.

I am going to live, William thought, coming out of Major Weasel's quarters. On the front line, with an injured leg, but alive. Who knows whether Carl Mühlegg has also been interrogated? William wondered whether he had lied, too.

Something had happened in that forest. William had found and lost the girl with the North Sea in her eyes. Who knows where she was now, at that moment. He had met a German soldier whom he had failed to shoot and who had failed to shoot him in turn; he had said goodbye to his friend the mouse. And he had left a room that had held him prisoner for too many years of his life – the room in which he had sheltered his guilt.

Outside the field hospital, William met Edgar Martin and apologised, explaining that he had got lost. But he did not tell him about the girl, or the North Sea, or Carl Mühlegg.

'My back was killing me,' Martin said. 'It was a real struggle to return, the others helped me.'

'Are you all right now?'

'They just finished changing my bandage and gave me some morphine. They should extract the bullet, but they say it's too risky to try that here. They want to send me home – imagine.'

'And what did you tell them?'

'That I'm staying. There's nothing for me at home.'

'Promise me you'll reconsider.'

'As soon as I get the chance to do something worthy of a medal, and a place in the army, I promise I will.'

'Edgar, when I got lost in the woods, Julius escaped.'

'Don't make a big deal out of it, soldier. He was just a mouse, there are hundreds of them here.'

William returned to the dormitory with his friend. Sitting on his bunk, he counted his belongings and put them away carefully. He updated the list in his notebook:

Soiled uniform and cap in poor condition, boots with service laces, aluminium cup, mug, a pen, a pair of blue underpants, watch, grey scarf, a belt, the notebook in my hand, name tag reading: William Turner, Private, camera.

He spread out his twenty-eight military postcards on the bed and looked at them for a while. He spread out the crumpled English flag and wrapped twenty-seven of the postcards inside it, keeping only one for himself. Then he hid the flag under the mattress.

On that one postcard he wrote:

Father,

We've never spoken much, but I hope we will start to when I come home. What happened to Mum was a terrible accident. We can spend the rest of our lives in blame, or we can accept that we did not choose the circumstances we find ourselves in. Perhaps life is nothing more than the way we react to what happens to us, and perhaps, we can try and find a new way to react to it when I come back.

Yours,
William

That night, William approached Father Adams, who was sitting at the edge of the camp with his bowl of stew, writing in his diary.

'Padre?'

'Private Turner, what brings you here?'

'I wanted to ask you something.'

The chaplain nodded.

'I was wondering if you have decided to forgive him.'

'Who?'

'God.'
'I've thought about it a lot and come to a conclusion.'
'What?'
'I'll give him one last chance.'

FOUR

Flanders, 1933

'YOU DIDN'T TELL ME what you did in the woods after you let William Turner go,' the boy said.

'I stayed there for a while, looking for that girl. She might have been injured. I wanted to help her.'

'Did you find her?'

'She must have been hidden very well, or she was already far away. I waited by the bush, thinking she might come back, but she never did.'

Almost twenty years had passed since that night, but Carl Mühlegg remembered it as if it were yesterday. He had waited to see if the girl reappeared, wondering how anyone could possibly be kept warm by the scrap of woollen blanket she had left behind. It was so cold. He had noticed a burnt-out candle on the ground, picked it up and put it in his pocket.

'You couldn't tell the whole truth either, could you?' asked the boy.

'I would have risked being shot, just like William Turner. The same rules applied to us. But my patrol comrade had already informed them that we had heard noises, that we had gone looking for the source.'

'It really was Hitler, wasn't it? From the way you described him, he seems like the man who's ruling us now.'

'Yes, it was him,' said Carl, lowering his gaze. 'Not everyone wants peace.'

'If William Turner had shot him when he had the chance . . .' the boy stammered.

'Life isn't built on "what ifs". Of course, he could have shot him. But he didn't.'

'You didn't shoot William Turner either . . .'

'See, if I'd met him on the battlefield, I wouldn't have given it a second thought, but in that forest . . . In that forest we were just two young men afraid of each other. Like William, I felt homesick and wondered why I had ended up fighting in that stupid war. When I found out that William was deserting, I understood. You don't know how many times I had thought about running away, too, but I never found the courage needed to see it through.'

'This morning you told me that William wasn't that brave either.'

'There's something that goes beyond courage. Do you know what it is?'

The boy rubbed two fingers on his cheek as though it might help him think faster.

'No, I have no idea. What?'

'Love.'

'He was so in love with that girl that he risked his life? And he had just met her . . .'

'Everything moves more quickly in war. Fear, love. A little human warmth can turn into a profound connection. It's ironic and sad at the same time. William had to go to war to understand that he loved his father. He wanted to save the girl and be reunited with his dad.'

'So, did he succeed? Did he escape again and reach the North Sea . . .?'

'He was about to return to the front line, just like me. And the things he did from that point . . . I'll remember them as the most important part of that entire war.' Carl paused: he had been so absorbed in the story that he had only just noticed that the sky had completely clouded over. He remembered the endless December rain almost twenty years earlier; it felt like a cruel twist of fate. The inn was a little less than an hour away, but if it started raining now, they would catch a chill.

'We'd better get going,' he said.

'It might not rain,' the boy said. 'Please finish the story first. What did William Turner do that was so important?'

'He showed me and many other men the way to peace,' said Carl, as he gazed up at the sky.

Flanders, 1914

THE WAR WAS SUPPOSED to end well before Christmas. It should have ended soon after it began, in the summer. But it was still going strong at the start of winter. The men who read reports, made lists, and debated the fate of the world from the safety of their offices had not expected this outcome. Governments on both sides had given the military all available resources to bring it to a halt, ideally with a victory. Their resources were soldiers, and there were plenty of them: poorly armed, poorly trained young men. At least they were still being fed.

The war would have ended long before Christmas were it not for the trenches. As far as William knew, Karel Cogge and Hendrik Geeraert had invented them, when they opened the sluices of the Yser River and flooded the land with the North Sea, blocking the invading armies. William had often thought about the excessive irony of God and Destiny: the Germans had wanted to reach the sea, but it was the sea that had reached them, and everyone else.

He walked over the salt-encrusted earth, supporting Martin. The morphine was wearing off. If Martin wanted to be a soldier again and fight on the front line, he had been told he would have to use what strength he had left.

And this is exactly what he had chosen to do. He saw no alternative. Some people's lives are like that.

Most of the soldiers halted at the second line to give their bodies time to heal. Only a few continued to the front line, which was already being manned by plenty of fit, healthy soldiers – at least according to reports, lists and numbers. Among these soldiers were William and Martin, heading across the trenches towards no man's land under Major Weasel's orders. This time they weren't scared: William was resigned and Martin hopeful. Fear mostly comes from the unknown, and now they knew just what to expect.

Once they arrived at the second line they said goodbye to Father Adams and made their way to *The Good Pillow*.

'What a stupid name,' said Martin.

'I agree, my friend,' replied William, trying to find two free bunks, or at least a dry corner. But he was unlucky. The two men ended up settling down in the trench itself, sheltering in small nooks dug out of the earth. They looked like burial chambers. Surrounded by mud and lice, cramped like caged animals, William and Martin waited for orders to come for the next attack from Sergeant Blackwood Jones.

But Blackwood Jones had no intention of launching a new offensive – at least, not for the time being. He had already executed three attacks, all unsuccessful: the latest one had been a few days ago. He knew that if he made a fourth mistake he would be replaced, and thus he adopted a principle that most of the world abided by: he who takes the initiative always risks failure, he who doesn't avoids danger altogether.

While Private Reagan was cutting his hair, the sergeant also realised that if he was shrewd enough, he could claim responsibility for any action that had happened to go well at the front. If he played his cards right, Blackwood Jones might become a good politician one day. He would give that some serious thought after the war; until then, he would perform his duties sparingly, just as soon as Private Reagan had finished trimming his moustache.

Reagan, who was a barber's apprentice before he became a soldier, had been put to work at the front, cutting hair and shaving the men's stubble. He liked it, even though his scissors and razor blades were blunt, and instead of a salon, he was surrounded by dirt and mud. When Reagan cut the men's hair he forgot about the war. He concentrated on the head in front of him, whether it was thick with hair or nearly bald, and began to cut. He was the only barber in the battalion, and went up and down the first, second and third lines.

When he was finished with the sergeant's moustache, Reagan walked past the makeshift shelters where William and Martin were trying to sleep. He greeted them with a nod and pointed to William's hair, saying, 'You could do with a good chop!'

William and Martin spent the afternoon of 21 December on lookout. Martin supported his aching back against the earthen side of the trench: the mud was packed vertically. William stared through his rifle, ready to shoot any German who fired, or even moved on the other side of no man's land. Shots came and went, but they sounded non-committal – mere warning shots fired into the air, to obey orders that were just as feeble. The rain and the cold had a dispiriting effect on the men on both sides.

That night William and Martin stayed wide awake, battling with the lice. William left the hole several times, trying to pick them off. He almost preferred the rain. Martin scratched his entire body, but the pain in his back limited his efforts.

After a sleepless night, around dawn, William lit the pipe the young professor had left him. If he ever made it home, he would find and read the best novel in the world. He was not used to smoking and he coughed frequently, but kept at it, watching the sky until the rain gradually stopped and the stubborn grey clouds – which had not budged for weeks – made way for blue sky and sunshine.

'Edgar,' said William. 'It's stopped raining.'

But Edgar Martin did not answer.

*

'Edgar, the sun's come out.'

William kept saying these words, but Martin's eyes were rolling in his head.

'Call the stretcher-bearers,' William yelled at the soldiers, but they were busy chatting and smoking. 'D'you hear me? The stretcher-bearers!'

'I'll go,' one replied, and sped through the tunnels. He had to find Tyler, who was playing cards with another soldier on the second line.

When Tyler came back with the emergency stretcher they kept at the front line, he nodded to the other soldiers to move off and make space.

He and William positioned the stretcher on a mound of earth and lifted Martin slowly on to it. Martin yelped.

'The hospital doctor insisted that he was sent home, but Martin said he was feeling better.'

'I know, Tyler.'

'That's what he told everyone, even in the hospital. He kept on saying it when they changed his bandage. Each time it was soaked in fresh blood.'

'What d'you think?' William asked, biting his lip.

'I'm not a doctor, Turner.'

'Then we need to call one right now.'

'Here?'

'Yes, here.'

'They didn't even dare take that bullet out of him at the field hospital.'

William slapped his neck. Lice.

'We have to get him out of here.'

'We'll only make it worse,' Tyler said.

'We have no other choice.'

They tried to move Martin again, but he was yelling in agony. William told him to hang on in there, that they had to put him on the stretcher. Eventually, he was hoisted on and the soldiers set off. Their boots kept sinking into the mud but at least the sun was on their faces.

The minutes ticked by and Martin's moans grew fainter. William assumed that his pain was so overwhelming it had dulled his senses, but when Martin raised a hand to get their attention, William realised that he was reserving what little energy he had left to speak.

'Put me down,' he said.

'We have to get you to the doctor.'

'Private, do what I say.'

William nodded. They placed the stretcher on sandbags, amid the bustle of soldiers coming and going from the front line.

Martin gestured to William.

William sank to his knees in the mud.

'Yes, Edgar.'

'Promise you won't take me away from here.'

'You'll die if we don't.'

'I already have.'

'You're still alive, Edgar, I promise you that. We'll get that bullet out of you.'

'The doctor told me.'

'What?'

'That if I didn't find a real hospital, it would be a matter of time. He wanted to send me back to England.'

William's eyes moistened.

'And you didn't listen to him.'

'I might have died of an infection before I even arrived,' Martin said. 'And if the bullet had moved even a little, I would have been paralysed.'

'You could have tried . . . Why did you stay?'

There was more pain than query in William's words.

'I tried my luck.'

'But why?'

'This is where I belong, William. I spent a lifetime doing everything I didn't want to do. Being someone I didn't want to be. And you know what? I've felt happier in this last month as a soldier than I have in my entire life.'

'You are definitely one of the greatest soldiers on the face of this earth, Edgar, I've no doubt about it.'

'And you never were, William.' Martin smiled. 'You would have done well to leave when you were in the woods.'

'How did you know?'

'Because friends understand these things.'

'What d'you want me to do now?'

'Tell Tyler not to take me away. Stay and keep me company . . . I may regain my strength yet, and if I do I'll go back to fighting with even more enthusiasm than before. And if the bullet gets . . . even deeper . . .' He paused, catching his breath. '. . . and it means I lose the little blood I have left, well . . . Take me to no man's land.'

'No man's land?'

'To die like a real soldier.'

William took the flask of rum from his pocket, unscrewed the lid and tilted it towards his friend's lips. Martin took a long sip. 'Better already,' he said. 'Much better.'

Tyler assured William he would stay with them, at least until other wounded men needed to be transported to the field hospital. But on that day, 22 December, there was hardly any firing on either side and no grenades were thrown into enemy trenches. British and German soldiers were exhausted from their last attack four days earlier, which had left even more bodies in no man's land, and from the weeks of rain. Many of them were feverish, and taking some time to regain their strength.

In the late afternoon, the Christmas parcels sent by Princess Mary were distributed to the British soldiers, alongside the packages sent by civilians. Many of them had gifts from their families.

William and Martin did not receive anything, Tyler was sent a postcard with Christmas wishes. But they were given

Ericson's parcel to share: news travelled slowly and his family hadn't yet heard their son was dead. The parcel contained dried bacon and cigarettes, and the razor Ericson had so wanted, as well as a football.

'Did they really send him a football?' said Tyler. Then he asked if he could have the razor; he badly needed it. William took the bacon and tucked it into his coat.

There was a pipe and some tobacco in Princess Mary's parcel, as well as cigarettes and a photo of her. William put them to one side; he could exchange them for food. Martin oscillated between moments of extreme agony and others when he seemed better, which gave everyone hope that he would recover; in one of Martin's better moments, William took a photograph of him.

That night, under the motionless constellations of stars, the temperature dropped to below zero. The soldiers' soaking wet coats – the sodden wool made them even heavier – froze.

By now Martin could not feel his legs, nor could he feel the cold and damp texture of his clothes, nor hear the gunshots that occasionally hissed over the trench like warning signals. In the middle of the night, he reached out his hand just far enough to touch William's arm. William was freezing, only semi-conscious.

'William.'

'Are you all right, Edgar?'

'Your lips are purple.'

'So are yours.'

'The time has come, soldier.'

'Are you sure?'

'Yes, it's what I want.'

William raised his head out of the trench. No man's land was completely silent – empty, apart from the bodies of the dead soldiers.

'All right, then.'

William grabbed some sandbags, piling them one on top of the other to build a makeshift ladder. He loaded Martin onto his shoulder and began to climb. He climbed until his upper body emerged from the trench, exposed to the enemy. He hesitated, unsure whether to retreat or continue. But Martin's increasingly shallow breathing warned him that he didn't have much time. He climbed onto another sandbag, pushed up from his knees and stepped out into no man's land. He took a few steps forward and gently brought Martin's body to the ground. A patch of earth emerged from the icy water. It's like walking on the sea, thought William. It's like the moment before battle, thought Martin. He closed his eyes and saw himself running towards the enemy trenches.

'Go back now, my friend.'

'I'll be just a few feet from you. I'll hear you if you talk to me.'

As soon as William climbed back down into the trench, a shot flew over his head, narrowly missing him.

*

On the morning of 23 December, the pumps had sucked out almost all the water from the trenches and any water remaining had frozen, hardening the ground. The lice and rats had scurried off somewhere, leaving the wretched men to the wretched spaces they had so miserably chosen.

A sense of despondency spread among the soldiers on the front line, and the soft moans of Martin lying a few feet away in no man's land reminded them how short life could be.

The soldiers on guard gathered in a huddle around William. Some had come to support their dying comrade; others, having learned of Martin's wish to die in no man's land, and thinking him insane, had wanted to know how it would end.

Martin, who had never received anyone's attention before he became a soldier, sensed the human warmth emanating from the crowd. He felt kindred souls all around him.

Sergeant Blackwood Jones joined them. During his morning inspection he had wondered what so many men were doing away from their posts. He approached the edge of the trench.

'Soldier, can you hear me?' he called to Martin. 'It's Sergeant Blackwood Jones.'

'Hmm,' Martin moaned.

'Was this your decision?'

Silence reigned in no man's land for an entire minute.

'Yes, Sergeant,' Martin finally replied.

'How can we help you, soldier?'

'By leaving me here.'

Blackwood Jones did not know what to think but he was aware that he needed to make a decision. William whispered a suggestion.

'Call the chaplain immediately,' the sergeant ordered.

He stamped his feet on the ground, as if the clatter of his boots on the icy mud might restore order to the offbeat rhythm of his thoughts. He had already made far too many decisions, none of which had led to anything good. He blew all the air in his lungs out through his nose, inhaled, and brought his hands to his sides.

'Soldier,' he said, calling once again to Martin.

'Yes . . . Sergeant.'

'I would like to reward your self-sacrifice with a medal for valour. I'll award it to you myself.'

'A medal . . .' squeaked Martin faintly; his voice had almost gone.

'It's a great honour.'

'Sergeant, that's always been my greatest wish.'

Blackwood Jones could only hear the last words of Martin's sentence, so faint that they seemed to be coming from far away.

'And so, you'll have your wish.'

Father Adams arrived shortly afterwards, breathing hard in icy breaths.

'There's not much time left,' William said.

The chaplain drew the sign of the cross in the air and clasped his hands together. Gathering himself, he said a prayer to the God he no longer believed in. The soldiers and their sergeant remained silent, saluting their comrade who had chosen no man's land as his last station on Earth.

When Father Adams finished, William rose from the trench to speak his last words to Martin.

'Edgar, did you hear that? You even got a blessing.'

Only the sound of the wind answered.

'Edgar?'

Edgar Martin's body, lit up by the sun, was no longer moving. Whether it had happened before Father Adams arrived, or while he was praying, William didn't know. He remained silent for a long time, trying to hold back his tears. That was his way of saying goodbye to his friend – impassive, like Martin himself would have been. Martin, the small fellow with the strength of ten men who had lived carrying crates and died as a soldier.

'And he, too, is gone,' Sergeant Blackwood Jones said impatiently. He turned to the soldiers, 'Back to your posts, the show's over.'

Father Adams stayed behind, writing a few lines in his diary before putting it back in his coat.

'So, how's it going with God?' William asked him.

'At midnight tomorrow Our Lord will be born again. I'll give him one last chance – my patience is limited.'

'Let's hope he makes up his mind.'

Adams nodded, unconvinced.

'We only had a short time together, Martin and I . . .' William's voice broke and he shielded his face with his hands.

'He came and left the way he wanted to. That was important for Martin.'

'I don't know, but I hope so. I believe so.' William let Father Adams rest a hand on his shoulder. Just then, a warning grenade exploded by the trench, causing a landslide in the earth nearby.

Father Adams was now convinced that if the Lord granted any protection at all, he would do so far away. He ran along the front line, eager to reach shelter as quickly as possible.

William waited to make sure there wasn't another explosion and returned to his hole in the ground. He needed to close his eyes, at least for a while.

He thought of Martin in no man's land, and of the young professor smoking his pipe. Of the girl with the North Sea in her eyes. Who knew where she was now, whether she was still afraid; he would be.

*

William had always spent Christmas Eve in his father's workshop. In the weeks running up to Christmas, customers would bring three times as many watches to be fixed or polished, so that they could show them off at church on Christmas Morning.

William would run from neighbourhood to neighbourhood delivering them, on foot or on his rickety bicycle until late in the evening.

They no longer put up decorations. That had been his mother's job, and somehow, doing it without her felt disloyal, as though he were replacing her.

They weren't used to replacing things. When customers arrived with a broken watch, William's father would always say, 'We'll try and fix it,' firm in his belief that a watch wasn't just an object but a keepsake, like other precious items we might own.

'If your watch stops, you'll stop wearing it. A good repairman will keep it on your wrist.' William's father had repeated this belief to him many times when he was a child.

William had never stopped wearing his mother's watch.

He looked at it, and no longer knew what to think. Can an object really keep a memory alive? The sound of his mother's voice calling him as a child had long since vanished from his memory. He only heard it in his dreams,

but even then, it was faint. Even her face had begun to
fade; he had only managed to hold on to it because he
had melded his memories with the few remaining photos
of her which his father had framed and placed on a shelf
in the shop. Without those pictures, his mother would
have disappeared from his memory altogether.

William wondered how much longer he would survive
the grenades and the cold. So many of his comrades had
died, like the young professor, and now Martin. William
would have liked to tell his father that one's memories of
people are kept most alive through the things one does,
not the things one gives up, and that he, too, had realised
this too late.

He did not come out of his dugout until late afternoon.
He asked for Father Adams, but no one had seen him. He
finally found the chaplain in a dormitory on the second
line; *Sweet Dreams*, it was called.

A mouse scampered off as soon as William entered. He
thought of Julius. He missed him, but he was glad to know
that he was far away from the fighting. He hoped this
other mouse would find a way out, too.

Father Adams was lying on a bunk, obviously tipsy. His
tunic reeked of beer. He must have dropped his cup, which
lay upturned on the floor.

'William,' he mumbled.

'I came to see how you are.'

'He doesn't exist, William. I've dedicated my life to a
God who doesn't exist.'

'What makes you think that? That he doesn't exist?'

'Oh, he should have given us a sign by now, and he
hasn't, he hasn't.'

'Maybe you missed it? Maybe something is going on out there right now, while you, Padre, lie half-drunk and moaning in here.'

'The Lord up there,' Father Adams said, pointing to the earthen roof, 'should be sending signals that we notice here, not *out there*.'

'So, what would you like to do?'

'As soon as I feel better, I'll go back to headquarters and resign.'

'But it's not a job.'

Father Adams reflected for a moment, but couldn't come up with a good answer, so he said nothing.

'Padre?'

The chaplain sighed. 'Tell me, William.'

'What if I asked you to keep trying for a little longer? Tomorrow is Christmas . . .'

'What should I do?'

'Give your blessing to me and my comrades on the front line, please.'

'I have no intention of going back there.'

'Not even for some bacon? You can have mine – I've no appetite.'

Father Adams' mouth watered. 'Just a blessing?'

'At midnight. That's all.'

'Ah, all right,' he said, pulling himself to his feet.

They made it to the front line – Adams stumbling over his own feet – just in time for dinner. They had also been promised a portion of pudding that evening.

An hour before midnight, the soldiers began exchanging good wishes and making toasts with beer and liquor that had arrived at the camp, in a token effort to lift their spirits. One of the men began playing a concertina. It was a sweet, gentle sound in the dark.

William took his place as lookout with a few of the other soldiers, as per Major Weasel's orders. He slipped his rifle through the barbed wire, pointing it at the enemy trench.

There was no movement on the German side, but he knew that this peace meant nothing. An attack could happen any minute.

William couldn't concentrate; the man with the concertina was now playing a Christmas tune, but he was more focused on Martin's body than on the enemy trench. It looked as if Martin was sleeping on the frozen ground.

'D'you hear that sound, Edgar?' he whispered. 'Christmas is about to come here, too.'

'Something is happening,' said a fellow lookout.

William clutched his rifle, his eyes on the enemy trench.

'Where?' he asked.

'There.'

'More to the right,' added another lookout.

'I can't see.'

'That light. We should warn the sergeant . . .'

'I'll go,' said another of the lookouts.

'Will you pass me the binoculars?' William reached out towards his comrade. Peering through, he saw there really was a light in no man's land, above the branch of a leafless tree which had broken in half just beyond the enemy trench. A faint, solitary light moving in and out of the darkness.

The soldiers on watch stayed stock-still and, after another minute or so, saw a hand emerge from the top of the trench, holding another light.

'D'you have any idea what they are?' one of the lookouts asked William.

'I think it's the sign the padre was looking for,' said William quietly.

'What sign?'

'They're candles.'

For a moment he thought he could see the North Sea, a frozen lake in no man's land.

The soldier on lookout sent for Sergeant Blackwood Jones; he arrived, his eyes blazing.

'Prepare the grenades,' he said. 'This time it won't be a warning. We'll send them all the way back into their trenches. Whatever they're doing, we'll put a stop to it.'

William pointed his binoculars at the broken tree. There were now four candles. In the trench, a group of soldiers were preparing to attack; the chaplain was gathering his things in a hurry.

'Father Adams,' said William. 'Maybe the sign has arrived. Down there.' He pointed to the German trench. 'Don't you see it – the North Sea? It's everywhere.'

'Are you all right, boy?'

'No, not at all,' William replied, leaping up over the trench and into no man's land.

William took a few steps and arrived at Martin's body. He slowly bent down and placed his rifle beside his friend's unmoving head.

'Will you keep this for me, my friend? I don't need it. I'm so tired of fighting, and so are our comrades. As far as I'm concerned, it ends here. Now. Tonight. Wherever you are, save a place for me. I'm sure you've already found a living forest where we can go and collect wood together.'

William faced the enemy and spread his arms wide in a sign of surrender.

Dozens of rifles and two machine guns were all pointing at him from the German trench.

*

William's boots cracked the thin layer of frozen earth. The candlelight seemed impossible to reach; it was so far away, and his bones ached. He looked down and imagined himself walking on ice. Can the sea freeze? He didn't know, and it didn't matter. He just wanted to move forward, one step and then another, all the way to the end of the world.

The soldiers from William's trench were making ready to launch their grenades. Sergeant Blackwood Jones had not expected this. He knew how he had to proceed with Private Turner, but the Germans would soon get rid of him anyway.

The soldier with the concertina had not seen what was happening and continued to play. His music sounded quietly across no man's land, drifting softly into to the enemy trenches.

William concentrated on the melody. He walked on, his leg dragging, his eyes closed. His mother was beside him; she had emerged from her white-walled room. And his father was there, too, smiling with his thin lips. He wasn't used to smiling, but he did now. And the girl with the North Sea in her eyes.

'Let's go, William,' she said. 'We can't stop now.' All the Germans saw was an unarmed soldier approaching them from no man's land to the sound of faint music. William was quietly singing a song. *Silent night* – his mother used to sing it to him – *holy night* – his voice grew louder. He knew that any moment now the Germans would give the order and gunshots would rip through his chest.

Alles Schläft, he heard a soldier sing in a strong German accent. *Einsam wacht*, another soldier continued, now joined by other voices.

William opened his eyes again and stopped walking. He was well beyond the halfway mark of no man's land.

A third soldier, his gun pointing at William, was standing above the enemy trench.

He slowly approached. William stayed still, waiting for him. Once the soldier was closer, he could make out his features clearly.

It was Carl Mühlegg.

'What are you doing? D'you want to get yourself killed? The officers are back there stuffing their faces, and my comrades want to know if you've gone mad. I offered to come and talk to you, since I speak your language.'

'Just like I told you in the forest, Mühlegg, I'm tired of the war. Tired of shooting at other men.'

'The candles are our only way of reminding ourselves that it's about to be Christmas. You see the one that's about to go out?' Carl Mühlegg pointed to the tree. 'When you left the forest that day, I recovered it from the bush. It belongs to the girl who was with you.'

'D'you know where she is?'

Mühlegg shook his head. 'She'll already be far away now. Maybe she's reached the North Sea, like you wanted.'

William began to smile.

'What do we do now?'

Carl Mühlegg lowered his rifle.

'I don't see any enemies here,' he said, laying it on the ground. 'Wicked folk don't have any songs.'

'What does that mean?'

'It's a German proverb. It means that I come in peace.'

Behind Carl Mühlegg, William saw an arm poking out from the parapet and arranging a fir tree with more candles on the edge of the trench. Another candlelit tree appeared further along.

'What are they doing?'

'They need some peace, too.'

William reached out his hand and Carl Mühlegg shook it.

'Englishmen!' he shouted. 'Come out!'

After a short silence, a voice answered.

'You first!'

A soldier with a drum strapped to his back climbed out of the German trenches. He inhaled deeply as he stood up in no man's land and took a few uncertain steps towards them. Another soldier quickly followed; he was carrying a flute. Then a third, who began to play his violin. He struck two out of every three notes, but still, that music sounded different from everything else around them. It was made of colour.

'You have a band,' said William.

'Improvised, but it's got some good parts. They were preparing a small Christmas concert.'

On the British side, the soldier with the concertina poked his head above the trench and joined in with the rhythm of the violin. He stopped playing just long enough to climb out of the trench. Then he resumed. The soldiers with the flute and drum played on.

Two more British soldiers climbed up into no-man's-land, laid down their rifles and made their way towards William. They were carrying jam and pudding, which they offered to Mühlegg.

'D'you smoke?' he asked them.

They nodded.

'Does anyone have cigarettes?' he shouted to his comrades. 'There's some delicious pudding here!'

A few German soldiers rushed to exchange cigarettes for jam and pudding. Others followed, then more and more. From both sides.

Sergeant Blackwood Jones came out of the trench as well, unsure whether he should celebrate or despair. Headquarters would send him to the firing squad as soon as they found out about this. He had to stop it. He went to talk to Mühlegg, glaring at William. But he was greeted with a bottle of liquor. He relaxed after a few sips.

'I'll have to tell them that I was in the back, that I knew nothing about this,' he mumbled, pointing to the bottle. 'Can I keep it?'

Father Adams was just above the British trench, watching the whole scene, clutching his rosary and praying in a low voice.

William went over to him.

'Here's your sign,' he smiled.

'It's been in front of me the whole time, actually.'
'Are you talking about the candles?'
'I'm talking about you, William.'

There were over a hundred soldiers gathered in no man's land, most of them in their early twenties. The darkness was complicit in their gathering, rendering British and Germans indistinguishable.

*

On Christmas morning, William asked Carl Mühlegg to help him dig a grave, and together they buried Edgar Martin's body. Martin had wanted to die in no man's land, and there he would remain. All the soldiers spent the early hours of the day burying the bodies of their other comrades, too, honouring their dead.

Father Adams enlisted the help of a small group of soldiers and set up the object he needed to hold a Mass between the two trenches. He gave a long sermon about signs – those we can see and those we can't. He put a lot of effort into his speech, but since he had not slept, and had drunk anything offered to him, his speech was slurred and only a few of the English understood what he was saying. He still received applause from both sides, and when he had finished the soldiers shook hands to honour this brief moment of peace.

Reagan brought two chairs, one for himself and one for anyone who wanted their hair cut; that was his gift. He cut hair all morning, and with each snip he felt closer to the day he would return home.

The men shared the food that had arrived in their Christmas parcels, and that was their lunch. In the early afternoon, an English soldier arrived with a football.

'Ericson's ball . . .' said William.

'We can play,' proposed a German soldier.

'Except the goalposts are missing.'

'Just a moment,' Tyler said.

He ran towards the trench, jumped down, and emerged with a stretcher. Three of his comrades helped him fix it to the ground.

The German soldiers did the same, and no man's land became a football pitch. Germans against Englishmen. Four stretchers as goals, the trenches as boundaries. Someone whistled and somebody else kicked the ball.

The soldiers began to play, sometimes falling into the craters made by exploded grenades. There were so many of them, it was hard to get their feet on the ball. After just a few minutes they were tired. But they kept going.

An Englishman scored the first goal, but the Germans matched it immediately; within a few minutes they had doubled their score. The English ran backwards and forwards, without any strategy – dozens of panting soldiers on a bare expanse of earth – breathing out warm breath that slowly evaporated in the cold air. After an hour, almost by chance, the ball bounced off the feet of a soldier who was taking a breather in the German goal, and they were equal once more. Five minutes before the end, a German scored the winning goal: 3–2.

'As soon as we get home, we'll give you a chance to get even on a better field,' said Carl Mühlegg.

'Deal,' William replied.

'How long d'you think it will take?'

'Not long at all, after what happened today. The war, for us, is over with this truce.'

William nodded vigorously. 'I think so, too.'

'Have you ever heard of Putzi? He was quite famous at home.'

'Never. Who is he?'

'A clown.'

'You have a clown soldier?'

'Over there. I think he's improvising a show.'

William and Carl approached the audience watching Putzi. He had placed a glass bowl on a table; it was filled to the brim with water. Two goldfish were swimming inside it.

'Where did he get that?' asked William.

'I have no idea. With Putzi, there's no point asking him any questions.'

Next to the bowl were three coloured rubber balls, silk handkerchiefs and a black magic wand. Putzi juggled the balls in the air, first with two hands, then with one. His other hand laid the silk handkerchiefs over the glass bowl. When he had finished this delicate operation, he threw the balls high into the air, and the men fought to catch them. Putzi called one of them over, and solemnly asked him to lift the handkerchiefs one by one as he rotated his magic wand. The soldier proceeded, and everyone remained silent. A suspended silence: the fish had disappeared. The clown jumped backwards, then forwards, touched his throat and spat up into the air twice. The goldfish came out of his mouth, drew an arc through the air and returned, alive, to the bowl.

'How did he do it?' asked William.

'It's Putzi – he doesn't reveal his tricks to anyone.'

'Did he make the comrade who was with you in the woods disappear? I didn't see him today.'

'He's gone. Apparently, he said that we were a disgrace to German honour and that we must return to battle. I'm not surprised, he's a strange type.'

William shrugged. 'I have to do something before it gets dark. There's not much time left.'

He took his camera and asked Carl Mühlegg to help him gather the other soldiers. Then he took as many photographs as he could. He knew no one would believe him otherwise, if one day he told the story of their Christmas.

As he framed the faces and prepared to take the photo, William realised that he had not had one taken of himself since arriving. He explained to Carl Mühlegg how the camera worked. He huddled into the group of British and German soldiers and looked into the lens, a cigarette between his lips.

It had never been their war, but the young men had not known that before they joined up. Now they did. No war belongs to those who fight it, William thought, as this Christmas drew to an end. There were no officers on the casualty lists, no government representatives, just the boys who no longer wanted to fight. When the officers and governments on both sides heard about this small moment of peace, they would probably have to surrender. The other soldiers, British and German, felt the same way; no-man's-land now belonged to them all.

William's eyes were downcast, but he was not sad. He was no longer sad. Soon he would leave, a free man.

He had kept the promise he had made to his mother. He had stopped the war and saved thousands of lives. Soon he, too, would finally reach the North Sea.

When darkness came, and the soldiers began to say their goodbyes with promises that they would stop fighting, three warning shots were fired into the air from the German side. The soldiers were startled, and most of them instinctively ran back to their own trenches.

Less than half of the soldiers, including William and Carl Mühlegg, remained in no man's land. They heard more shots whistle over, inches from their heads this time.

'The officers must have returned, William. I doubt they took it well.'

'Carl, I'm glad I didn't shoot you in the woods.'

'I'm glad, too.'

'Wait . . . Take this.' William handed him his watch.

'Are you sure?'

'I don't need it any more. You keep it. I didn't get it before, but now I know . . . The only road we can follow is that of living in the present.'

'I'll remember that,' said Carl Mühlegg. 'Merry Christmas.'

'See you on the other side of the North Sea.'

They nodded to each other – their time was up – and each of them ran back to his own trench.

When William was safely back with his own side, he looked out on to no man's land. All the soldiers had gone. The first snowflakes had begun to fall from the sky.

All that was left out there was a table with a glass bowl full of water.

And two goldfish, swimming.

FIVE

Flanders, 1933

THE BOY BANGED THE soles of his boots against the earthen bank. He looked around and imagined hundreds of soldiers huddled together in the rain and the cold. There was a big field in front of him, covered in grass, on which lush beech and chestnut trees were growing. That field had once been no man's land. The place where William Turner and his father had stopped the war.

'Did he really tell you all the things you just told me?'

'Yes, in the forest, and on Christmas Day in 1914. I know it sounds strange, but before we said goodbye, we both understood that we had become friends. We promised to stay in touch and see each other again if we made it home safely.'

'And how was it? When you saw each other again?'

Carl Mühlegg remained silent, searching for the words.

'We never did, son,' he said. 'The next day orders came in from headquarters. Anyone who had fraternised with the enemy would be sent to fight elsewhere, far away from Ypres. There were too many of us to be punished by firing squad, and so they settled for hiding the truth. A few eyewitness accounts were published in English newspapers, from letters soldiers had sent to their families, but the machine of war was too powerful and it made sure that these rumours were dismissed as lies. It was even worse here in Germany – not a single article came out about it. The war went on for another four years. And in Ypres alone, over a million people died.'

The boy mulled over that number – a million – then lowered his eyes.

'I can't think of such a big number.'

'It would be like Munich and all the inhabitants of villages like ours disappearing.'

'Terrible,' the boy said, thinking of all those young men who had left home, never to return.

'And what happened to William Turner?'

'When the war ended, I looked for him, for God knows for how long. I had heard that he fought for another two years, but after 1916 all trace of him was lost. He seemed to have disappeared from history. What's certain is that no one ever had any news of his return. I like to think that he is resting here, together with his friend Edgar Martin, and that the girl with the North Sea in her eyes still comes to visit him from time to time.' Carl held out his wrist. 'All I have left of him is this watch, which he gave me before returning to his trench, and an old photo.'

Carl pulled out a newspaper clipping from his pocket.

'Look – the one with the cigarette in his mouth, that is is William.'

'He looks sad, like he's deep in thought.'

'Not at all. He was so happy that day. He had kept his promise and made peace with the past. All he could think about was reaching the sea and boarding a ferry with that girl. He wanted to be in England in time for them to celebrate his father's birthday.'

'And this photo?' the boy said. 'It's from a newspaper. Which means that he managed to develop them.'

'Shortly after the Christmas truce, Father Adams managed to get himself sent back to England with the camera that William Turner had left in his care before being transferred. The chaplain held on to it for years, waiting for William to come back and claim it. Time passed and William never appeared. Eventually, he developed the reel. Only a few photos were saved, including this one, which I took. He sent them to a newspaper, but William Turner's story got lost in headlines about other matters. It was just one of the many anecdotes about the war.'

'Did you meet Father Adams?'

'I managed to find him.'

'Really? And where is he now?'

'In a tiny village near Salisbury, south-west of London. He told me that every Christmas, during Mass, he tells the story of our truce. Few believers listen to him, but he's happy anyway. He's convinced that if even a few people know a story, there's a chance they'll pass it on.'

'What about you? Did you stay in the war, Dad?'

Carl pointed to his stump.

'For another year. I almost lost my life a few times, and William Turner always returned to my thoughts. I wanted some of his courage. I never found the strength to escape. So I made another choice. One day, at the start of an attack, I shot my own hand. I couldn't fight with one hand, so I went back to Germany and stayed there. That's when I met your mother – in the hospital. She was a nurse at the time.'

'I miss her. I hope we can see her soon. Tomorrow's Christmas Eve.'

'We'll be with her tomorrow and we'll celebrate Christmas together.'

'Promise?'

'I promise,' said Carl. 'Are you hungry? It's getting late.'

The boy was very hungry.

'Let's go back to the inn, then. But first we must do one more thing, and I'll need your help.'

Carl removed the watch that had once belonged to William Turner.

All those years he had been wondering what he should do with it: whether to take it to be repaired, or lock it in a keepsake box, as one sometimes does with memories. After embarking on his journey to find Father Adams and then meeting him, he had set out again to find the watch shop. He had done some research and had collected numerous addresses of possible shops. Finally, in one, he'd found William Turner's father bent over his workbench. He was hunchbacked, and seemed much older than his years.

Carl had introduced himself, explained who he was and that he had a story to tell. The story of the man's son. The man had hung a sign on the shop door and locked it with a double turn of the key, saying, 'I'm listening.'

And he had listened, without saying a word. For several hours, Carl told him the story William had told him in the woods, and all about Christmas Day. William's father remained impassive the whole time; it seemed as if he did not even need to breathe. Only his eyes, towards the end, had filled with tears, as if something, somewhere inside him, had finally resurfaced.

Carl had unfastened the watch from his wrist and placed it in the hands of William's father. He examined it with the expertise of someone who had dedicated his life to repairing them.

To Carl's surprise, William's father returned it to him.

'The only way forward, young man, is the present.'

'Pardon?'

'That's what my son said to you on Christmas Day, when he thought he'd be coming back to me soon, right? You know I would have liked to see him walk into the shop with that girl, after they had crossed the North Sea together, but instead all I'm left with is a postcard. I lived in the past for a long time. I lost a wife, and then a son. Look at me now . . . I'm an old man. Carl Mühlegg, you said your name was, didn't you?'

'Yes.'

'Keep my son's words close. You still have many years ahead of you. If something bad happens in your life, don't bind yourself to the past, like I did. Instead, keep moving forward. Every one of us has a sea to aim for.'

'I'll keep it in mind.'

'Before you leave, I'd like you to make me a promise.'

'Of course,' said Carl Mühlegg.

'Take this watch back to my son's resting place. So that he has a little of his mother and father beside him.'

Now, Carl Mühlegg was searching for the exact spot where he and William had said goodbye, but so many years had passed, and the place looked so different now.

'It should be here, more or less,' he said to the boy.

'Let's go for it.'

Using only their hands, they dug a small hole. Carl was slower than his son, but then, he only had one good hand to work with.

'D'you want to do it?' Carl asked his son.

He handed over the watch, and the boy placed it in the loose earth and gently scooped over fresh soil.

'We can go now,' said Carl, placing a pebble on top. 'I don't want us to get caught in the downpour.'

On the walk back, the boy stayed close to his father, silent, pulling his coat tightly around him against the cold wind, thinking.

'That's why I'm called Wilhelm, isn't it?' he asked.

His father tousled his son's blond hair.

'Yes, Willi. That's why.'

When they arrived back at the inn, the innkeeper greeted them with bread and a bean stew. The boy ate greedily, his eyes fixed on his plate. Then they returned to their room and gathered up their few possessions.

'Shall we leave that here?' asked the boy, pointing to the candle on the windowsill. 'It will light up the nights of those who come after us.'

Carl paid the bill and they set off again on the path on which they had arrived, just the day before. The first snowflakes began to fall as they walked. Just as they had so many years ago in no man's land.

'There's one thing I don't understand.'

'Tell me.'

'What use was William Turner's action if the war just carried on?'

'It showed us that peace is possible, if we want it.'

Carl looked up. Great snowflakes were falling now, and the fields were turning white. He told his son that they would stay in Ypres for one more night before setting off in the snow again.

'We're not going home again, are we?' the boy asked.

'No. There's no place in Germany for a family like ours. Besides, home is wherever the three of us are all together.'

'Where are we going, then?'

'Towards the North Sea,' his father replied. 'Your mother is waiting for us on a beach. From there we'll go to the docks and board a ship. To America.'

The boy lifted his head. He tried hard to imagine what was going to happen and how his world was going to change, but he couldn't yet make sense of it.

He decided, instead, to have faith.

Letter from the author

The idea for this book came to me in the summer of 2019, while hiking in Asiago in the Italian Alps. Those mountains contain the remains of military fortresses and what remains of the trenches of World War I. I had been told about them, and I knew that many young soldiers had lost their lives, but I had never actually seen them. While there, I met a man, a semi-retired history professor, who told me he spent every summer visiting the trenches of World War I. It was the kind of serendipitous encounter that happens when you go walking alone in the mountains.

'People who come here don't know that they are walking on the dead,' he told me. 'Thousands and thousands of boys are buried in these lands.'

The professor spent the evening telling me about the trenches he had visited in Europe, of those he had yet to visit, and of soldiers and armies that had barely made history, or not at all.

Then he told me a story I had never heard before: the Christmas Truce. In 1914, in Flanders, both the English and German armies met unarmed in no man's land, like brothers, to celebrate Christmas.

The more I listened to him, the more I wondered how all those soldiers had suddenly chosen to lay down their arms. I wondered about the man who took such a courageous and monumental initiative. Before we parted company, he made a comment which has ever since haunted me: '*We must be careful because history repeats itself.*'

By mid-October, the Christmas Truce was still in my head. I called the professor and asked him to recommend reading material on the event.

I began with *All Quiet on the Western Front* by Erich Maria Remarque, which showed me how to narrate war through the lives of people who maintained their humanity in desperate circumstances. I also found Peter Englund's *The Beauty and the Sorrow* helpful. I read anecdotes and battle techniques, in more technical books such as *The British Army in World War I* by Mike Chappell and *Stormtroop Tactics: Innovation in the German Army, 1914–1918* by Bruce I. Gudmundsson. Another book that helped me better understand the psychology of those who choose to fight is *War as an Inner Experience* by Ernst Jünger.

But the book that had the most impact on me was *Der Kleine Frieden im Großen Krieg* (*The Small Peace in the Great War*) by German journalist and biographer Michael Jürgs. As I read it, I felt intimately connected with those young men immersed in the muddy trenches, but I still did not know how to draft the story as a novel; there were too many characters. The question for me remained: who was responsible for the truce, and why? What kind of a person would break all rules, defy orders, and endanger his life by trusting his enemy? William Turner, a nineteen-year-old English volunteer.

While asking myself the second question – why anyone today would care about a minor event during World War I – the pandemic hit Italy.

I live alone in a small apartment, with a six-square-metre back porch, from which I can barely glimpse the sky. In isolation (albeit a comfortable one, with food, heating and electricity), I read and reread letters soldiers had written from the front, in Alan Cleaver's book *Not A Shot Was Fired: Letters from the Christmas Truce 1914*.

In reconstructing William Turner's story, I have tried to be as faithful to the facts as possible, but I have also had to fill in gaps. In addition to William Turner, there were others: Father Adams, 'Greeter' Foster, Sergeant Blackwood Jones, and above all Carl Mühlegg, the German soldier who met William Turner on the battle-field. There is no evidence that Hitler was present for the Christmas Truce, but nor is there evidence that he was not. And he had certainly known about it. Hitler was a dispatch runner for regimental headquarters during WWI, and his unit was in Ypres between 29 October and 9 November 1914. I changed the names of some soldiers; other characters, like the Girl with the North Sea in her Eyes, I invented. Unlike the soldiers, she did not choose war, and did not want to leave her homeland. Carl Mühlegg in the present (1933) is my own invention, as is William Turner's past, his internal war, and his guilt after his mother's death.

As I wrote this novel, I, too, was fighting my own demons nourished by isolation. After the first chapters, I realised that it was not only William Turner who had stopped the war. No. It takes two.

My point is this: an unexpected and meaningful meeting of two men who chose to lay down their arms is anything but little. Even though they are largely forgotten, and did not change the fate of the war, their actions carry a fundamental message from which we can learn profound lessons.

By putting down our weapons, both real and imagined, we can aspire to live in a better world.

After finishing the novel, and days before delivering it to my publisher, Russia brought war to the gates of Europe. Was the professor right? Was history repeating itself?

Peace on the Western Front is not, however, a novel about war. It speaks of peace on every page, and I would like to leave its readers with a sense of empathy and hope. We are not condemned to repeat the future, but to change it.

This is a list of texts I read while researching my novel.

Bibliography:

History
–   Antonio Besana, *1914: Qualcosa di nuovo sul Fronte Occidentale.*
–   Cataldo Bevacqua, *La tregua di Natale di Ypres.*
–   Mike Chappell, *The British Army in World War I (1): The Western Front 1914–16.*
–   Bruce I. Gudmundsson, *Stormtroop Tactics: Innovation in the German Army, 1914–1918.*
–   Ernst Jünger, *War as an Inner Experience.*
–   Michael Jürgs, *Der Kleine Frieden im Großen Krieg*
–   Eric J. Leed, *No Man's Land: Combat and Identity in World War I.*

- Nigel Thomas, *The German Army in World War I (1): 1914–15*.

Biographies
- Alan Cleaver, *Not A Shot Was Fired: Letters from the Christmas Truce 1914*.
- Peter Englund, *The Beauty and the Sorrow: An intimate history of the First World War*.
- Mike Hill, *Christmas Truce by the Men Who Took Part*.
- Bruce Bairnsfather, *Bullets & Billets*.
- Bruce Bairnsfather, *Fragments from France*.
- Ernst Jünger, *Storm of Steel*.
- *Edith Wharton's Writings from the Great War*.

Fiction
- Erich Maria Remarque, *All Quiet on the Western Front*.